"It seems to be the event of the season.

Connor's dry tones twisted the knots in her nerves even tighter, so that before Jenna had time to think she had swung around, switching on a blatantly false smile.

"So isn't it a pity that you won't be here to see any of it?"

"I might decide to stay around—see the show."

"What do you want? Was the new shop just an excuse? You've really come back to cause trouble.... No?" She ended on a note of disbelief as he shook his dark head adamantly.

"There's no need for any trouble. So long as you agree to have dinner with me."

"You must be joking!" Rejection flared in her eyes.

"No joke, Jenna," he assured her. "You asked what I wanted—the simple truth is that I want *you*."

KATE WALKER was born in Nottinghamshire, England, but as she grew up in Yorkshire she has always felt that her roots were there. She met her husband at university and she originally worked as a children's librarian, but after the birth of her son she returned to her old childhood love of writing. When she's not working, she divides her time between her family, their three cats and her interests of embroidery, antiques, film and theater and, of course, reading.

Books by Kate Walker

Kate Walker

SATURDAY'S BRIDE

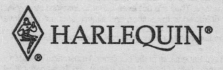

TORONTO • NEW YORK • LONDON
AMSTERDAM • PARIS • SYDNEY • HAMBURG
STOCKHOLM • ATHENS • TOKYO • MILAN • MADRID
PRAGUE • WARSAW • BUDAPEST • AUCKLAND

ISBN 0-373-12131-8

SATURDAY'S BRIDE

First North American Publication 2000.

Visit us at www.eHarlequin.com

Printed in U.S.A.

CHAPTER ONE

THE lift came to a smooth, silent halt, its doors sliding open without a sound. Jenna Kenyon stepped out into the elegant foyer of the exclusive George Hotel, glanced round her briefly, then froze in stunned horror.

The warm, contented smile fled from her lips, all colour leaching out of her face. Shock turned the normally brilliant emerald of her eyes to a deep, shadowed green, and her cheeks looked almost white in contrast to the soft fall of her dark brown hair around her oval face.

Please, no! she thought frantically. Please let it not be true!

Let it be just an illusion, a fantasy, some trick of the light! Please let her mind be playing games with her so that she hadn't really seen what she thought she had!

Fate really couldn't be *that* unkind, could it? It wasn't possible that she should be forced to come face to face with the man she least wanted to see again in the whole world. Particularly now, when everything had seemed to be going so well. When her life was well and truly back on an even keel, and it seemed that peace and happiness were within her grasp.

Blinking rapidly to clear her blurred vision, she forced herself to focus once more on the tall, dark-haired masculine figure at the reception desk. It was a struggle not to give in to the overwhelming urge to let her gaze skitter away, look *anywhere* but at him. It had to have been a mistake. Just someone who looked vaguely like him—she really couldn't be that unlucky!

But her luck was well and truly out. A second and then a third, even less willing glance revealed only too clearly that the man now taking his key from the receptionist was none other than Connor Harding, the rat who, just over five years before, had shattered her life and then walked away, leaving her to pick up what little was left.

'Any messages?'

And if she had had a single remaining doubt then the sound of that deep, faintly husky voice would have driven it away in a second. She could never forget that voice. Never lose the memory of how seductively it had whispered to her in the darkness of the night, the soft, treacherous lying words he had spoken.

'None, I'm afraid, Mr Harding.'

The receptionist sounded genuinely cut up about it too, Jenna reflected cynically, as if she really cared. No doubt she had fallen an easy prey to the brilliant, devastating smile Connor could turn on with such lethal effect. It disarmed anyone in seconds, and had susceptible women falling almost literally at his feet.

As you did, she reproached herself bitterly. You were as gullible as anyone; more so. You let him into your heart, into your bed. He could do as he wanted...

Well, not any more!

With a hard mental shake, Jenna pulled herself up sharply. It was time she got out of here—before Connor noticed her presence. Already he was turning to follow the porter to his room—using the lift.

Panic warred with a blazing sense of anger, making her heart lurch into a ragged, uneven pounding that sent colour flying into her face, her breathing jerky and unnatural.

If he saw her...! The last thing she wanted right now was any sort of scene in so public a place. Frantically she hunted for some form of protection, anything to hide her face.

The sheaf of papers in her hand provided the answer. Silently offering up a prayer of thanks for the seemingly endless lists of things to do that her mother had insisted on giving her that morning, she turned away carefully and bent her head over them, running a pen down the page as if checking them off.

She knew the moment that Connor walked past, sensing his presence in the air as a cat becomes aware of an intruder into its territory. There was a waft of some expensive after-shave, a soft laugh in response to something the porter had just said, the firm tread of fine leather shoes on the tiles.

But at a deeper, far more instinctive level there was an almost primitive recognition of his closeness, a shivering sensitivity that lifted all the tiny hairs on the back of her neck. The instant antipathy mixed shockingly and inexplicably with a devastating physical hunger that hit low in her stomach and held her frozen until the sound of the lift door closing smoothly behind her told her that he had gone.

Thank God! Jenna let her shoulders sag in the rush of release from tension as she turned towards the door. She couldn't get out of there quickly enough. And if tomorrow her mother thought of anything else that needed attending to, she could do it herself. That, or send...

'Miss Kenyon!' A voice hailed her, loud and clear, from the doorway of a nearby office. 'Just a moment!'

It was the hotel's deputy manager, Paula Barfoot. In her late fifties, she was tall and elegant in a navy pinstripe suit and high-heeled patent leather shoes, and over the past weeks she had made the Kenyon family's wishes her personal crusade.

'I'm glad I caught you! Was everything all right for you today? Is there anything you need?'

'Everything's fine,' Jenna assured her. 'The function room will be perfect, and the menus you suggested sound delicious.'

'So you're all ready for Saturday, then?'

'Just about. Oh—there was one thing I wanted to discuss with you. My mother has decided to change the seating arrangements yet again. Do you have a minute to go over the details?'

'As long as you need. How about coffee while we talk?

Sarah...' she addressed the dark-haired receptionist '...coffee for two, in the conservatory, please. This way, Miss Kenyon.'

It was as she turned towards the large Victorian-style conservatory that overlooked the hotel gardens that a sudden sixth sense, a shivering frisson of awareness slid down Jenna's spine, warning her that all was not well. With a nervous, jerky movement, her head snapped round towards the lift, where she had last seen Connor Harding.

He was still there! The sound of the doors closing had lulled her into a false sense of security.

But perhaps she was worrying too much. Maybe he hadn't heard Paula call her name. Even as the thought entered her mind she knew she was only fooling herself.

'Miss Kenyon...' The deputy manager was at her elbow again, clearly bemused at her delay.

But Jenna couldn't drag her eyes from the man by the lift. A man who now stood so still, his dark head turned in her direction, his deep blue eyes watchful and alert but revealing no trace of anything that could remotely be described as emotion. His frozen stance reminded her of a hungry predator, scenting its prey close at hand and waiting for the optimum moment at which to launch itself into the hunt.

And now those cruel hunter's eyes were turned in her direction, narrowing unnervingly in fierce recognition. The cold sweep of his blue-eyed gaze over her, from the top of her sleek mane of dark brown hair and down her tall, slim body in the stone-coloured cotton shirt and loose trousers two shades darker, had a brutally assessing quality about it that made her blood run cold in her veins.

And the brief, condescending inclination of his head in belated acknowledgement of her presence did nothing at all to appease her disordered feelings. If anything, it only made matters so much worse, coming far too late for any sort of politeness, and being too calculatedly indifferent to be any indication of friendliness.

Jenna had never been subjected to anything so icily hostile in her life. She felt as if the wordless antipathy that seemed to throb in the silence must reach out and engulf everyone there, beating against their temples as it now pulsed inside her head, making her want to lift her hands before her face in an instinctively protective gesture.

'Miss Kenyon?' Paula said, on a very different note, one that made her realise that the way she was standing, frozen into stillness like this, was having the exact opposite effect of the one she had hoped for.

She had wanted to creep away quietly. Instead she had drawn the attention of all eyes, and had totally ruined any chance of escaping without Connor ever realising she was there. Now everyone here had seen that Jenna Kenyon and Connor Harding had come face to face again after all this time. And if the small town's gossip grapevine was its usual efficient self, that fact would be the topic of fascinated discussion at every supper table by tonight.

'Miss Kenyon?'

'I'm so sorry!'

Switching her attention to the older woman with an effort, she forced herself to turn her back on Connor and direct a smile into the deputy manager's face. She was grateful that Paula had only recently come to the George, and so knew nothing at all about the Harding-Kenyon feud and her own and Connor's shared history.

'Coffee would be lovely.'

She might not be able to *see* Connor any longer, as she followed her escort into the conservatory, but she could feel his cold-eyed gaze on her as she walked away. It burned into her spine like a laser, making her almost believe that she would be branded with its imprint for her life.

Five years had done nothing to lessen the impact he had on her, it seemed. She had hoped that time might have blurred it at the edges, or dulled its power, but, recalling with a sense of nausea the clawing hunger that had assailed her when he had simply walked past, Jenna had to acknowledge miserably that it had done no such thing. Even a deeply rooted, burning hatred of him could do nothing to reduce her shivering response to the tall, hard body, every muscle still as honed and tight as when he had been a trained sportsman.

'I'm not surprised you couldn't take your eyes off our visiting celebrity,' Paula Barfoot confided as they settled in a couple of chairs cushioned in turquoise and gold. 'If I was fifteen years younger I could fall for Connor Harding myself.'

'What's he doing here?' Jenna struggled to make the question sound casual. She would have thought that Connor's new status as a millionaire businessman would have kept him well away from the small town in which they had both grown up. Certainly, in the past, he had been only too keen to shake the dust of Greenford from his shoes without a backward glance.

'Haven't you heard? Oh, but of course; I forgot that you don't live locally any more. Harding's are opening a major store in the new shopping precinct, and as Greenford is Connor's home town he decided to attend the event himself. I'm sure there'll be a lot of media interest—it's not every day we play host to one of the country's top sporting heroes.'

'He hasn't played tennis for years,' Jenna pointed out. Not since he had broken his leg in a terrible fall.

'More's the pity!' Paula's eyes sparkled with appreciative glee. 'I can't be the only one who used to watch Wimbledon just to see him in his shorts—those thighs! But now he moves in a very different sort of world—just as successful, of course, if not more so.'

Which explained the sharply tailored suit, the expensive luggage and the exclusive hotel, Jenna reflected. Connor Harding had made his first fortune in prize money and lucrative sponsorship deals when he had been Britain's number one tennis player, but in the five years since he had retired from the sport he had more than doubled that amount by sound investment and astute business acumen. The string of sports outfitters he now owned all over the country was just part of his highly successful and profitable empire.

'Now, tell me what the problem is with the seating arrangements and I'll try to sort it out for you,' Paula went on, reverting to their original topic of conversation. 'Of course you want everything to be just right for Saturday. A wedding should always be perfect, just the way the bride imagined it in her dreams.'

'Excuse me, ladies…'

The sound of the deep, masculine voice sent a shudder down Jenna's spine, every nerve tensing in instant recognition. Sitting up stiffly in her seat, long lashes veiling emerald eyes, she forced herself to face Connor's enquiring midnight-blue gaze with something approaching a degree of calm.

'Did either of you drop this? I found it in the foyer.'

Jenna knew at once that the small black purse was not hers, but she still went through a pretence of checking in her bag in order to give herself an excuse to turn away. The few moments' grace was an opportunity to draw a deep, reassuring breath in order to ease the unsettled racing of her heart.

'Not mine,' she declared sharply.

'Nor mine.' Paula's response was quieter, less abrupt. 'Why don't I take it and put it in the safe in the manager's office? Then if anyone asks at Reception they'll know where it is. If you'll both excuse me?'

'I'll keep Miss Kenyon company till you return,' Connor suggested, with what Jenna privately considered excessive courtesy.

'Oh, do you two know each other?' Paula was obviously intrigued. *You didn't tell me,* the hint of reproach in her glance at Jenna communicated, without a word.

'We—were at school together for a while,' Jenna supplied hastily, anxious to play down the connection.

'We were a lot more than that,' Connor inserted, deliberately stirring things up again. 'But we haven't seen each other for—how long is it, Jenna? Five years? Six?'

'Then I'll leave you to talk over old times.'

Paula clearly thought she was being tactful, making herself scarce. Watching her go, Jenna had to bite down hard on her full lower lip in order to catch back the urgent plea not to be left alone that almost escaped her.

'Would you like to do that, Jen?' The soft mockery in Connor's voice combined with the wicked light that danced in his eyes to set her teeth on edge. 'Shall we talk over old times? Reminisce…?'

'You know that's the last thing on earth I'd want to do!' Jenna tossed back, in what she hoped was a coldly quelling manner.

Unfortunately Connor appeared totally unconcerned by the icy bite in her words, or the fulminating glare she turned on him. Sliding his long body into the chair opposite, he leaned back comfortably, with every appearance of being prepared to settle down for a long, intimate chat.

Seeing him up close at last, she could not be unaware of the changes the years had brought. There were a few extra lines that fanned out from those amazing eyes and around the sculptured shape of his mouth, and his face had lost any lingering touch of boyishness, becoming all man, but nothing dramatic.

Time had been kind to him, but then the clean, carved lines of his handsome face owed everything to the sort of forceful bone structure that the passing years would never change. The long, straight nose and arrogant jaw would remain whether he was thirty-one or seventy-one, and those stunning eyes, thickly fringed with black lashes, and the sensual curve of his mouth were exactly the same as when she had first come close to him over fourteen years before.

There was a small, silvery scar, faintly marring the line of one straight black brow, that hadn't been there before, but she didn't allow herself to wonder how he had come by it. She didn't want to know anything about his life in the time since he had turned his back on her, leaving her alone and desolated.

'Go away!' she breathed furiously, her fingers clenching over the handle of her coffee cup as she fought the temptation to fling its contents straight into his darkly taunting face.

She had never thought she could feel like this. Never before had she been at the mercy of a purely primitive rush of sheer blind fury that was like the buzz of adrenaline in her veins. She could see it in Connor's eyes too, in the savage yellow flames that blazed in their navy depths.

Unspoken aggression seemed to play around them like a wild electrical storm, taking her out of her normally controlled and sedate self and into new and unknown territory. And after years of hiding her feelings, of pretending that she had healed, that she had forgotten the unforgettable, it was a wonderfully liberating feeling to experience something so basic, so uncontrolled.

'Leave me alone or I'll…'

'You'll do what, Jenny Wren? Call the manager and have me thrown out? I think not. This isn't Greystone Hall and I'm no longer the local bit of rough who wasn't fit to kiss your pretty feet. I rather suspect that you might find that *you're* the one asked to leave and not to trouble the guests.'

He could be right about that, Jenna admitted unwillingly. The controlled excitement in Paula's voice, her deferential attitude towards Connor, told their own story. That liberating sense of anger departed in a rush, leaving her feeling limp and deflated like a pricked balloon.

'And I see no sign of the Brothers Kenyon lurking in the wings, ready to do your dirty work.'

'I don't need my brothers to back me up!' Jenna flashed in angry protest.

'Then things *have* changed!' Connor returned with dry irony. 'I thought the Kenyon Three were always on guard duty where their little sisters' honours were concerned.'

'My brothers have lives of their own to live. As do I. Things haven't stood still since you left Greenford, Connor. You're not the only one who has moved on—and away…'

'You're still here.'

'But only temporarily. I don't live in Yorkshire any more.'

The flicker of surprise he couldn't quite hide went some way to restoring her sense of mental balance. So he hadn't expected that!

What *had* he thought? That she would stay at home for the rest of her life, nursing the wounds he had inflicted on her and never venturing away from the security of her family home? She had to admit that at one point the idea had held distinct appeal, but if she had given in to that weakness then he would have won.

She had almost died because of this man—both literally and emotionally—and, looking back, the emotional pain had been harder to recover from than the physical distress. But she *had* recovered, and she wanted him to know it.

'My work and my home are in London. I'm only here for the week.'

'For the wedding.'

So he had overheard Paula's comments. She hadn't realised that they had been audible to him from where he had been standing.

'Yes, for the wedding.'

'And when is that exactly?' It was impossible to interpret his tone, to read anything in his carefully opaque blue eyes.

'On Saturday, at Saint Giles's.'

'Of course. Where else? And…'

The rest of his words were drowned out by a high-pitched call from the doorway.

'Jenna! Yoo-hoo! Jenny!'

'Oh, no!' Jenna groaned under her breath as she recognised the elderly lady in the bright pink suit and extravagant purple lace and net hat who was now bearing down on them. 'Not now!'

'Your aunt, I believe,' Connor murmured, his mouth taking on a wry twist.

'Great-aunt, actually,' Jenna corrected automatically, getting to her feet with obvious reluctance.

She had no alternative but to face this out, even if at this particular moment she wished her elderly and decidedly vague relation back in the comfortable sheltered housing in which she usually spent her days. Normally she was very fond of her great-aunt, but right now Millicent Kenyon was almost the last person she wanted to see.

'Jenna, poppet!' An exuberant air kiss slid past Jenna's cheek; her great-aunt's attention was on the man with her, who had also risen politely to his feet. 'How lovely to see you! Won't you introduce me to your friend?'

If only there was some way she could say no, Jenna reflected privately. But there was no getting out of this.

'Connor Harding, Miss Kenyon,' Connor put in with impeccable courtesy. 'Would you like to join us?'

'Oh, I can't stop.' Millie's disappointment was written all over her face. 'I'm having lunch with Hazel Mortimer and I'm already running late. But I saw this dear girl and I just had to come over and say hello. Are you here for the wedding, young man?'

'I'm afraid not.'

Connor's smile held a touch of conspiratorial appreciation of the way Jenna choked faintly at her aunt's term of address. Still, she supposed that from Millie's advanced years anyone under forty would seem to deserve the description of 'young'. She could only be grateful that the old lady's unreliable memory had not yet latched on to the name Harding, and all the problems it brought with it.

'I'm only in town unexpectedly. Jenna and I lost touch with each other some time back, and we met by chance a few moments ago.'

'Connor has to leave Greenford before Saturday,' Jenna put in hastily, suddenly overwhelmed by panic at the thought that her great-aunt might just decide to issue an invitation herself.

'What a pity. Oh, well…'

Then, just as it seemed she was about to depart, just as Jenna had allowed herself to relax and let the breath she had been holding on to out in a deep sigh of relief, the older woman turned a wide, beaming smile on her.

'But more importantly, my dear, how's Saturday's bride?' The question was accompanied by an exuberant hug. 'Everything organised for the big occasion? Any last-minute nerves?'

'Everything's under control,' she managed, with an ease that was a long way from the way she was really feeling. Her pulse was beating in double-quick time, so that she was sure Connor must hear the hectic thud of her heart as it pounded inside her chest, and she knew that the accelerated response had sent a wild colour flooding into her cheeks, betraying her inner turmoil. 'I've just been checking on the arrangements here, and it all seems perfect…'

'But of course it would be. The George is such a superb hotel—the sort of place that can handle a society wedding with style and efficiency. I must say I'm really looking forward to the big day. And how is the handsome groom? What was his name, now?'

'Graham,' Jenna supplied unevenly, still avoiding Connor's blue eyes. 'Graham Dixon.'

'Graham, that's it! A lovely boy! He—'

She broke off as her attention was diverted by a call that came from the doorway. Glancing in the direction of the sound, Jenna spotted another woman of her great-aunt's age waving energetically.

'Isn't that Hazel, now?'

'So it is! Well, I must love you and leave you, my dears. So nice to meet you, Mr Harding. It's such a pity you'll miss the wedding, but perhaps…'

'Aunt Millie, your friend's waiting,' Jenna inserted hastily, fearful of what might follow.

'I must fly, then! Goodbye, my darling, see you on Saturday.'

Watching her great-aunt's departing back, Jenna was forced to wonder whether what she felt was relief at having averted a potentially explosive situation, or a strong sense of apprehension at the thought of what might follow. In order to avoid one difficulty, had she in fact jumped from the frying pan well and truly into the fire?

'It seems that Saturday's wedding is to be the event of the season.'

Connor's dry tones twisted the knots in her nerves even tighter, pushing her into unguarded action, so that before she had time to think she had swung round to face him, switching on a wide, blatantly false smile.

'So isn't it a pity that you won't be here to see any of it?'

The smile wavered, fading rapidly before the cynically enquiring lift of that scarred eyebrow.

'I might decide to stay around—see the show.'

'You wouldn't be welcome!'

Connor's sensual mouth twisted dangerously before curling into a devilishly taunting grin.

'The days when I had to ask permission of the Kenyon clan before I so much as breathed are long gone. I do as I want now, and no one—*no one*—gets in my way.'

'Is that a fact?' Jenna had to swallow hard to ease a throat that had become painfully dry, making her voice croak embarrassingly on the words. 'What *do* you want? Was the new shop just an excuse? You've really come back to cause trouble...? No?' she ended on a note of disbelief as he shook his dark head adamantly.

'There's no need for any trouble,' Connor told her quietly, but the softness of his voice did nothing to disguise the dangerous undercurrents that lurked beneath the apparently innocuous words. 'So long as you agree to have dinner with me.'

The cool audacity of it, his obvious conviction that all

he had to do was ask and she'd fall in with his plans, took her breath away. No, he hadn't even asked. It had been a command, pure and simple, ruthless and unyielding in its indifference to her feelings.

'You must be joking!' Rejection flared in her eyes, flashed like lightning across a darkened sky.

'No joke, Jenny Wren,' he assured her, with complete disregard for her indignation. 'You asked what I wanted— the simple truth is that I want you.'

'You…you…'

Words failed her completely as blind fury hazed her thoughts with a red cloud. Her hands clenched into impotent fists at her sides as she struggled against the impulse to lash out and wipe the easy smile from his face, drive the tauntingly smug expression from his eyes.

'How dare you?'

'It's only dinner, Jenna,' Connor put in smoothly. 'Do you always overreact so strongly to an invitation to a meal?'

The obvious pleasure he took in having wrong-footed her incensed Jenna even further, so that she actually stamped her foot in fury. She knew only too well that he had meant her to interpret his words in a very different way, and she hated herself for having fallen so easily into his trap.

'We're old friends who haven't seen—'

'We're nothing of the sort! And I don't want to have dinner with you! I can't even begin to wonder why you should invite me.'

'Can't you, Jenny? Can you really not see what's happening here? Do I have to spell it out?'

'Yes, I'm afraid you do. Because I haven't got the faintest idea just what's going through that devious mind of yours.'

She wanted to go on, say more, but Connor's softly spoken, 'Very well,' dried the words on her tongue. And a moment later all coherent thought fled as he did something that absolutely terrified her.

If he had moved sharply, making a violent gesture or grabbing at her, she would have flinched away, possibly turned and run, jolted into fleeing like a startled bird sensing the approach of a hunting cat. But Connor did nothing of the sort. Instead he reached out, the action very slow, very gentle, and let his hand rest on hers, warm fingers touching her skin so very lightly.

The sound inside Jenna's whirling head was like the buzzing of a thousand disturbed bees, making her thoughts spin. The heat of his flesh on hers seared across every nerve with the force of a potent electrical charge, so that she actually feared she might be branded with his fingerprints burned into her skin. Her throat dried painfully, her heart jolted inside her breast, and she couldn't stop herself from closing her eyes in swift, instinctive response.

She had barely completed the gesture when dark intuition warned her of the fatal mistake she had made, the way she had betrayed herself. Immediately her lids flew open again, in frantic rejection of her feelings.

Too late. He had been watching her all the time, dark blue eyes locked onto her face, the burning intensity of his gaze noting every tiny flicker of emotion, every trace of response she had been unable to hide.

'You see,' he murmured in that gentle, almost tender voice that brushed so softly against her nerves it sent shivers of reaction all the way down her spine. 'You see, it's all still there between us, as it was before. It's all just below the surface, waiting, needing just a spark, just a touch, to set it all off again, to turn it once more into the burning, raging hunger we once knew.'

No! Jenna wanted to scream. No, there's nothing there at all! You're deceiving yourself, imagining things! There's nothing between us—it all died years ago, shrivelled away to ashes when you walked away and never looked back.

But she knew she couldn't form the words. Even inside her own head they sounded hopelessly weak and unbelievable. Besides, Connor had seen her reaction, and she knew he would simply laugh in her face if she tried to deny her response.

So instead she grabbed at the only thing she could think of, clutching in blind panic at the one escape route her whirling, desperate mind threw at her.

'You're forgetting about Saturday! About the wedding. About Graham.'

The speed with which he reacted, the violent look that came over his face, the way he snatched his hand back, as if just touching her contaminated him, brought some small satisfaction to her disordered thoughts.

'You're right,' Connor said, and his voice was like the snarl of a predatory tiger. 'I was forgetting about the wedding. But never again. I shall make a point of remembering that only too clearly in the future.'

And as he stalked away Jenna was forced to wonder just how he had managed to make what seemed an acknowledgement of defeat and withdrawal sound so much more like the most deadly threat.

CHAPTER TWO

'AT LAST!'

Jenna sighed with relief as she ticked off the final point on yet another checklist. She had dealt with every single query and alteration her mother had thought up this morning, and now she could go home.

She couldn't get out of the hotel quickly enough. All the time she had been in the banqueting suite she had felt as if she was looking over her shoulder, fearful that at any moment Connor's tall, dark figure might appear in the doorway. As a result her nerves were painfully on edge, making her as jumpy as a nervous cat.

But thankfully there had been no sign of that lean, muscular form, no sound of that husky, attractive voice to torment her by raising unwanted, disturbing sensations deep inside her. She hadn't allowed herself to wonder whether the unsettled, jittery feeling that plagued her was the result simply of nervousness or something more inexplicable.

Surely she couldn't be *disappointed* at Connor's non-appearance? Rationally, she would have said that seeing him again was the last thing she wanted, but honesty forced her to acknowledge unwillingly that rationality had nothing whatsoever to do with the way she was feeling. Her emotions came from the most instinctive, most basic part of her. A part she had thought locked away long ago, but which Connor had been able to drag back into wild, uncontrolled life simply by the lightest touch on her hand.

'I'm out of here!'

'Talking to yourself, Jenny Wren?'

The lightly mocking voice caught her on the raw, making her spin round violently to stare in shocked disbelief at the man in the doorway. Yesterday's elegant suit had been replaced by a white tee-shirt and soft denim jeans that hugged the firm lines of his toned body with a sinful sensuality, drying her mouth in a response that was a uneasy mixture of fear and appreciation.

How had he known just when she was about to leave? Had some malign sense of intuition led him here at the precise moment when she was about to make her escape? Or had her own foolish thoughts conjured him up like some dark demon coming to torment her?

'Don't call me that! You know I always hated that stupid nickname!'

'There was a time when you used to ask me to say it.' That taunting voice had dropped an octave, becoming tormentingly soft and seductive.

A time when she had believed that he used it in affection—more than that, when she had been able to convince herself that he really cared, that he wasn't just using her as her brothers had claimed he used every woman.

'We all make mistakes when we're young and stupid. Thank God we usually grow out of them before anything too dreadful happens.'

'Is that what we were? A mistake?'

'What we *were*...' she emphasised the word starkly, hoping he would get the message loud and clear '...was one of those totally inappropriate affairs that ignorance and over-active hormones drive adolescents into before they develop better judgement. Call it a learning experience, if you like.'

'And what did it teach you?'

An intent light in those cobalt eyes made her shift awkwardly from one foot to another. To her annoyance her palms were damp with nervous perspiration, and she wiped them surreptitiously on her blue linen dress, catching them awkwardly on the buttons that went all the way down the front.

'That even the most civilised of us can sometimes be at the mercy of their animal appetites.'

The scowl that darkened his handsome face, turning that sensual mouth into just a thin slash of anger, made the blood run cold in her veins.

'There's one thing at least that the animals can teach us,' he shot back with blazing cynicism. 'They take great care of their young.'

Which stabbed straight to the heart of her own distress. So much so that she couldn't hold back a gasp of pain and shock and had to duck her head to hide the bitter tears that leapt into her eyes.

'And you'd know so much about it!'

'Did you give me a chance?'

'A *chance*!' Jenna's dark head came up sharply, green eyes blazing as anger burned away the tears of a moment earlier. 'You had every chance a man could want—and then some! So don't accuse me of not playing fair with you.'

'With me, perhaps, but not—'

But Jenna had had enough. Memories she had thought she'd finally managed to bury had once more worked their way to the surface of her mind, beating against her skull with a force that made her head reel.

For all that the June sun shone brightly through the huge windows behind her, she felt as if she was back in another, long-ago night, when the rain had slashed down and the thunder had roared. The remembered physical pain was so intense that she longed to fold her arms around her body, as if to hold herself together.

'No! I don't want to listen! I *won't* listen! That part of my life is over—finished! And believe me, I was never so glad as when I shut the door on it.'

'I'll bet—' Connor began, but Jenna refused to let him continue.

'And now, if you'll excuse me, I have things to do.'

Was that cold, tight voice really hers? She didn't recognise it, but at least it had the effect she wanted. Eyes burning, beautiful mouth clamped tight shut, Connor stepped back to let her move past him to the door, sketching a cynical mockery of a bow as he did so.

'Of course, you have to prepare for the event of the year. For your wedding to the glorious Graham.' The words came out on a vicious sneer. 'So where *is* the wonderful groom?'

For the space of an uneasy heartbeat the question caught her off guard, so that she frowned uncertainly. But then she recovered and said hastily, 'At work, of course.'

'Really? I would have thought that he'd stay glued to your side, going through all the arrangements with you.'

'Don't be silly!' Jenna switched on a tight, obviously insincere smile. 'He can't afford to take any more time off when he's already booked three weeks for the honeymoon. And he trusts me to take care of everything.'

It was an effort to move slowly, not to make it look as if she was desperate to get away from him. The few steps it took to get out of the room seemed to take an age, and she felt as if she was in a film that was being played out in slow motion as she reached the corridor and headed for the lift.

Hurry! Please hurry! Her finger jabbed nervously at the button to bring it down. In spite of herself, her foot tapped restlessly on the thick crimson carpet, betraying her anxiety to be gone.

Left to herself, she would probably have taken the stairs, but the uncomfortable suspicion that Connor might follow her ruled out that choice. She couldn't bear to think of being forced to continue this conversation any longer. As it was, he was behind her, the unwanted closeness of that tall, powerful body raising all the tiny hairs on the back of her neck in instinctive rejection.

'What floor are you staying on?'

She asked merely to fill the taut silence that stretched her nerves almost to breaking point. The answer to the question held no interest to her, except, perhaps, to reassure her that he wasn't likely to follow her on her downward journey.

'The ninth—the Balmoral Suite.'

She should have known. This new, affluent, sophisticated Connor Harding would only have the best that money could buy. And the Balmoral Suite was the *very* best the George had to offer. Taking up the whole of the ninth floor, it was the size of a more than average two-bedroomed flat and provided the ultimate in luxury—at a price. But at least that meant that he would be going up several floors, and so she would soon be free of his disturbing company.

'I'm sure you'll be very comfortable—' She broke off awkwardly at his cynical snort of laughter.

'Why not say it, Jenna?' Connor's sardonic tone matched the mockery in his eyes.

'Say what? I don't know what you mean.'

'It's written all over your pretty face. How things have changed when Connor Harding—the only descendant of the man your grandfather ruined—is able to afford to install himself in the most exclusive suite in the—'

'I wasn't thinking that at all!'

Angry defiance flared in her eyes. But even as she spoke the memory of that much younger Connor, the boy she had first encountered when she had been little more than a child, rushed into her mind, swamping the anger and extinguishing it as quickly as it had arisen. Her voice was less certain as she continued.

'You know I always believed that the feud between our families was the most ridiculous over-reaction.'

At first they had laughed at it, shaking their heads at the idiocies of the grown-up world. The fact that generations of Kenyons and Hardings had persisted in hating each other just because a grandfather on either side had fallen in love with the same woman had seemed almost farcical to them. And the resulting business machinations, which had pitted family against family in a bitter financial war, had seemed an even greater waste of time and energy.

It hadn't been until much later, when they had come to realise how deeply adult feelings like love and desire could take root, that they had had any understanding of how Abel Kenyon must have felt when Arthur Harding had enticed his bride away only weeks before their wedding.

Or at least Jenna had understood. Looking back, with painful hindsight, she had to admit that Connor had probably not felt any such thing. He had only pretended to be going along with her adolescent fantasies, his own emotions being much shallower, and far more basic.

He had wanted her in his bed, nothing more. And in order to achieve that aim he had been prepared to indulge her romantic imagination, which had seen them as a modern-day Romeo and Juliet, for just as long as it suited him.

'But that was before you made it personal.'

To her intense relief the lift arrived at just that moment, and she rushed thankfully into it as soon as the doors swished open, pressing the ground floor button on her way in. It was only a matter of seconds before the doors slid shut again, but those seconds were enough for Connor to follow hot on her heels, leaning back against the mirrored walls of the compartment as it began its descent.

'Before I made what personal?' he demanded harshly.

'I thought you said your rooms were on the ninth floor!'

Jenna's voice came and went like a faulty radio. This was precisely the scenario she had most dreaded, and the rapid, uneven pounding of her heart made natural breathing impossible.

The confined space of the lift emphasised the height and strength of his body, exaggerating its potent sexuality with a force that was like a blow to her heart. And the way that arrogant face was reflected all around her, its dramatic image repeated over and over in the glass of the walls, made her feel as if she was spinning out of control.

She seemed to be caught up in a pulsing spiral of delirium that blurred all thought, obliterated everything else but

Connor, and the memory of how much she had once
wanted him.

'You'll need to go back up again,' she managed weakly,
struggling to gather together the shattered remnants of her
thoughts in the hope of distracting him from her foolish
reaction.

But Connor simply ignored her quavering speech.

'Before I made *what* personal? That damned feud? You
forget, my lovely Jenna, it was your brothers who did that.
If they hadn't interfered, then—'

'Then what? It would all have been sweetness and light,
and we'd now be playing happy families together?'

But of course he couldn't go that far.

'Not that, no...'

'Of course not that!' she flung at him bitterly, tossing
her head and sending the dark waves of her hair flying out
around her. 'You never thought that— Oh!'

Her tirade snapped off on a cry of shock and fear as the
lift compartment suddenly made an appalling noise, shuddered dreadfully, and screeched to a violent halt.

Caught off balance, Jenna was flung forward, completely
out of control. With a terrible sense of inevitability she saw
her own reflection in the opposite wall come dangerously
nearer, and she closed her eyes in panic at the thought of
the awful certainty of hitting it painfully.

It didn't happen. Instead of the bruising impact of her
body against the glass she felt herself caught and held securely in a strong grip. A pair of muscular arms enclosed
her and she was brought up hard against the firm, warm
lines of a man's chest—Connor's chest, obviously, because
there was no one else it could possibly be.

She could feel the softness of his tee-shirt under her
cheek, the strength of the powerful ribcage beneath it. His
heart beat steadily and calmly, unlike her own, which was
racing in double-double time. When she caught her breath
on a shaken sigh, the clean, musky scent of his body enclosed her, so that just when she had thought she might be

able to stand on her own her legs seemed to weaken again, making her sway against him.

'Are you all right?'

'I—I think so. What happened?'

If her voice had been wobbly before, it was practically non-existent now, and not just from reaction to the dramatic change in their situation.

'I don't know. The lift just stopped—some sort of technical problem, I suppose.'

He sounded remarkably unconcerned, so much so that a blazing shaft of suspicion shot through her, stiffening her spine and bringing her head up sharply. Green eyes glared up into his dark face, sparking with accusation.

'Some sort of technical problem?' she echoed sceptically, her tone making it plain she was not so easily deceived. 'Remarkably convenient, if you ask me! What have you done?'

'Done?' Those stunning eyes opened wide in a display of pained innocence that might have convinced a weaker heart than her own. 'Jenna, what a suspicious mind you have! But I'd better try and do something now. Can you stand on your own?'

'What?'

Belatedly Jenna became aware of the way he was still supporting her, her upper body resting against his, her breasts crushed against the wall of his chest.

'Oh, yes, of course.'

Hot colour flooded her cheeks as she pushed herself away, clumsy hands coming up to straighten her clothes, smooth down a skirt that suddenly seemed to end somewhere around the tops of her thighs, exposing a thoroughly indecent length of smooth, creamy skin and slender leg.

'I'm fine! Just do something to sort this mess out.'

But already Connor had returned to his original position, lifting the emergency telephone from its rest on the wall.

'Hello? Is there—? Oh, hi... Yes, I hope you *can* help me...'

He listened intently for a moment, his mouth twisting wryly at something.

'Yes, I'd appreciate that. We'll just sit it out, then—we don't seem to have much option. She says there seems to be some sort of problem with the lift,' he told Jenna on a dryly satirical note as he replaced the receiver. 'That much we'd sort of gathered.'

'So what are they going to do?'

Determinedly Jenna ignored her conscience's demand that she should apologise for her earlier suspicions.

'Try and sort it out. She said it may take a while; the engineer's on his lunch-break so they'll have to go and find him.'

'And what do we do in the meantime?'

'All we can do is sit it out. As I said, we don't have any other option. We might as well make ourselves comfortable...'

'Oh, no!'

The thought of spending just the short time it took to reach the ground floor in the confines of the lift with him had been bad enough. The prospect of being cooped up with him for even longer was almost unbearable. The worrying suspicions she had had earlier about Connor's motives now returned in full force.

'I can't! I *can't*.'

'What's the problem?' Connor's blue eyes probed her face, the sharpness of concern not quite concealing some other deeper, darker emotion, one that sent a sensation like the trickle of icy water down her spine. 'You're not claustrophobic, are you?'

'No.' Jenna's eyes slid away from his, unable to bear their fierce scrutiny. 'But...'

'But nothing, Jenna. We're stuck, and the only thing we can do is make the best of it. Now, are you going to sit down? Because I'm sure we would both find it more easy to relax if we did.'

CHAPTER THREE

IT WAS the firm, reproving, schoolteacher's voice Connor used that finally convinced her she had no alternative. That and the casual way he flung himself down onto the carpeted floor, his back resting up against the wall, long legs sprawled out in front of him. He certainly did look much more comfortable that way. And surely if he did have any ulterior motive he wouldn't appear quite so indifferent as to whether she followed his example or not.

'All right.'

Reluctantly she lowered herself to his level, finding it almost impossible to settle herself comfortably while maintaining some degree of modesty. If she curled her legs up, the tight skirt of the linen dress rode up high on her thighs, and sitting cross-legged like a child would be even worse, just the idea making a rush of hot colour flood her cheeks. In the end she adopted a position that matched his, with her legs stretched out in front of her, but keeping them tightly together and stiffly straight in stark contrast to Connor's relaxed indolence.

'Settled now?' he enquired, when at last she gave up twisting and turning and sat still. He had watched her adjusting her position with obvious amusement, but she was thankful that he spared her the mocking comment she felt sure was close to his lips.

'Perfectly,' she retorted sharply, and clearly untruthfully. 'So what do we do now?'

'Well, the options seem rather limited.' That amusement still lingered, setting her teeth on edge. 'So unless you have any more interesting ideas, I suggest that we talk.'

'Talk about what?'

Connor's broad shoulders lifted in a shrug of casual indifference.

'Whatever you like. Saturday's wedding seems the obvious subject.'

'I'd rather not,' Jenna muttered uncomfortably.

'Really? You surprise me. I would have thought that it
was the subject uppermost in your thoughts—that any
woman would just love to talk about the preparations for
her marriage to the man she loved. But if you prefer then
perhaps we should consider other possible topics—like recalling old times...'

A bite of acid slid into his voice, draining it of all warmth
so that the words fell like ice on Jenna's exposed skin.

'Remembering how it used to be when we were together.
How we—'

'All right! What do you want to know?'

Anything was better than letting him rake up the silt of
old, bitter memories. Memories that tore at her heart just
to think of them, that she would die rather than expose to
his merciless, cruel assessment. She could just imagine how
he would shred the few tiny illusions she had left, leaving
her mentally raw and bleeding as before.

'Tell me about your fiancé. About the gorgeous Graham.'

'I wish you wouldn't call him that!'

'Why? Isn't he gorgeous? Are you claiming that you're
going to marry someone who looks like the Hunchback of
Nôtre Dame?'

'Not at all! It's just that he's...'

In her mind she pictured Graham's face. Grey-eyed,
topped with thick, dark hair, it was a gentle face, a warm
face. Graham wasn't gorgeous in the way that you would
say Connor was, but he was...

'He's nice!'

'*Nice!*' It was a snort of contempt. 'Nice? What sort of
a description is that?'

Hastily Jenna tried to cover her tracks, snatching back
the ground she had lost.

'Niceness is a very underrated quality these days. Too many people take it to mean dullness or ordinariness, but to me it's worth its weight in gold.'

The look Connor slanted her was one of cynical scepticism, making her wonder anxiously if she had protested too much. But the critical comment she nerved herself to hear didn't come. Instead he adjusted his position slightly, so that he was facing her more directly, and continued as calmly and easily as he might have done if they had just been introduced to each other at some social function.

'What does he do?'

'He works in a bank here in Greenford. They've just made him Manager of Personal Banking. It's a great promotion seeing as he's only thirty-three.'

Her voice faltered, died on the recollection that by the age of twenty-six Connor had already retired from one career in which he had reached championship level and set himself to building up a whole new one in the business world. Already a millionaire, he had long since increased that fortune several hundredfold, and now, at thirty-one, was still two years younger than Graham.

'And do you love him?'

'I'm very fond of him.'

As soon as they were out, she recognised the mistake she had made and wished the foolish words back. But too late. Connor pounced on them with the fierce alacrity of a hunting cat, his voice a cruel purr as he tossed them back at her.

'*Very fond.* That's not enough! Do you really intend to sign your life away to this man on the basis of "very fond"?'

'I'm not signing my life away—you make it sound like a business deal!'

'No, *you* make it sound that way! Graham's *nice*,' he sneered. 'You're *very fond* of him. Bloody hell, woman, the only thing you've got excited about so far is the fact

that he's had "a great promotion" at the bank! Why are
you marrying this man if—'

'It's enough for me!'

Jenna felt as if she was precariously balanced on the edge
of a dangerously high cliff, buffeted by a biting wind as
she scrabbled desperately for a foothold. It would take just
a tiny push and she would fall over, heading for who knew
what danger on the rocks below.

'What else would I want?'

'What happened to passion—desire? To the hunger you
can't control?'

Connor abandoned his indolent position as he pushed
himself upright so that he was half-sitting, half-kneeling in
front of her. Navy eyes locked with green, holding her gaze
transfixed so that she couldn't look away, couldn't even
blink to break the hypnotic contact.

'What about the need for another person that's so strong
you think you'll die if you can't be with them? Do you feel
that for your "nice" Graham?'

*I felt that for you, and it nearly killed me when you
turned your back on me. On me and the unborn baby I
carried inside me.* The pain was like a scream inside
Jenna's head. *The baby you never wanted, never acknowledged, except as a barrier to the success you wanted so
desperately. I knew that hunger for you, that need, and it
destroyed my life when I lost you. Do you think I would
ever willingly go through it again?*

She would never know how she overcame the impulse
to fling the desperate words into his darkly watchful face.
Only the certainty that he wouldn't care, that they would
slide off the armour of his indifference without even leaving a mark, held her back. Instead, using a control she
hadn't known she possessed, she drew a deep, calming
breath and forced herself to speak with a composure that
was the exact opposite of the way she was feeling.

'I tried passion once. Once was enough. I had more than
my fill of it. Passion hurts, it destroys—it kills!'

The last word came out on a hiss of such vindictiveness that she had the dubious satisfaction of seeing his head go back, as if her words had been some deadly poison that she had spat in his face.

'That hunger you call desire is just a primitive force, nothing more. Why hedge it round with careful words when a very simple one will do? It's *lust*, that's all. And lust is very definitely a four-letter word in my vocabulary!'

'At least it's an emotion that's stronger than the milk-and-water affection you claim to feel for your Graham. So tell me, is that why you don't wear his ring?'

'Wh-What?'

'His ring!'

Connor pounced on her left hand, snatching it up and holding it between them in a firm grip that splayed her fingers apart.

'If your Graham is so special, then why don't you want the world to know it? Why don't you wear his ring proudly so that anyone can see? Why don't you flaunt it in my face and tell me to go to hell, that you have another man now, one who wipes out the past, obliterates everything there ever was between us?'

'I—I...'

Jenna knew she was totally adrift now. She had plunged right to the bottom of the cliff and into the dark and dangerous waters below. She was drowning, very definitely going down for the third time, with the icy waves threatening to close over her head.

'I—we—we don't need that sort of—'

'Don't give me that rubbish, Jenna!' Connor brutally dismissed her stumbling attempt at explanation. 'It's not good enough and it never will be—and you know it!'

'Not good enough for what?'

'To cancel out what there was between us—what there still is.'

'No.' It was a sound of desperation, and even in her own ears it had no strength, no force to make it a true denial.

'Yes!'

Connor's grip on her hand changed, easing, loosening, becoming almost gentle as he turned it so that his fingers totally enclosed hers, drawing her towards him with a soft but irresistible pressure that pulled her back away from the wall, brought her white face to within inches of his.

'Jenny, don't do this—don't deny what we have—don't deny yourself.'

As he spoke his lips brushed her forehead, her cheek, and Jenna could only moan in weak despair as the brief, warm caresses triggered off the wild, pagan longing that she had thought she'd buried long ago.

But she hadn't buried it deep enough. Certainly it hadn't stayed buried. Instead it seemed that, as Connor had claimed the day before, it was all still there, just below the surface, needing only the tiniest spark to set it alight. In the space of a couple of uneven heartbeats the heat was pulsing through her veins, flooding her skin with warmth, with excitement, with that hunger she had tried to deny.

And it was hunger that was uppermost as her mouth sought his, fastening on it with the greed of someone who has been starving for too many long years and is now presented with a glorious banquet. Her fingers clenched over his arms, clutched, clung, then slid with unrestrained eagerness into the dark tangle of his hair at the nape of his neck.

'Jenny!'

It was a sigh of delight, of dark satisfaction, breathed against her mouth. But a moment later even that sound was choked off as the pressure of his lips forced hers open, his tongue tangling with hers in the heady, provocative teasing that mirrored another, far more intimate invasion.

The kiss went on and on, driving her to madness, stripping all thought of restraint, of control, from her mind. She was adrift once more on a wild sea, but where the other had been icy, and darkly treacherous, this one heated the temperature of her blood and carried her higher and higher with every glorious, tempestuous wave that crested and broke over her.

She didn't know if Connor fell backwards or deliberately moved so that he was lying on his back on the carpeted floor, but she went with him willingly, her body coming down on top of his, breasts crushed against his chest, her hips lying in the cradle of his pelvis. The heat and hardness of his desire reached her even through the layers of their clothing, and he moaned in sensual delight as she adjusted her position slightly.

'Made it personal!' he muttered, in a voice that was thickened and rough with hunger, an unsteady vein of shaken laughter running through it.

'What?' Jenna frowned her confusion.

'You accused me of making it personal. Oh, God, Jenna, how could it be anything else? It was always personal between us. Always was and always will be. Oh, come here, woman, and kiss me again!'

Jenna needed no second urging, lowering her mouth to his with a greedy alacrity that made him twist sharply underneath her. Rough, urgent hands moved over her body, caressing, exciting, awakening every nerve to heated, pulsing life so that she matched him touch for touch, sliding her own palms down his ribcage to the point where a heavy leather belt encircled his narrow waist.

A couple of quick tugs pulled the white tee-shirt loose, a sigh of ecstasy escaping her as she felt the heated smoothness of his skin, the slight roughness of body hair. The hunger that spiralled through her was sharp as a pain, beating at her thoughts, pulsing at the most intimate point between her legs. She felt she couldn't bear it any longer, so that when Connor's searching fingers finally found the buttons that ran down the front of the blue linen dress she could not hold back an inarticulate, choking cry of delight.

The few seconds he took to wrench them from their fastenings seemed like an aching lifetime to her, but at last she felt his touch on her skin, hard fingers cupping and supporting the weight of her breasts. Unable to control her response, she flung back her head in abandoned excitement, exposing herself to him. And Connor took full advantage, his mouth against the smooth, creamy curves, drawing one nipple into its heat.

'Oh, baby!' he muttered against her skin. 'I want you...'

Baby. The single, starkly emotional word slashed through the heated delirium that possessed Jenna, extinguishing it with the speed and force of icy water landing on flames so that she froze, glazed eyes staring straight ahead.

Baby! How could she forget what such wantonness had led to before? How could she have let him drive from her mind, even for one second, the repercussions that had followed from such mindless passion?

'Jenna?'

Connor had sensed her withdrawal. Cobalt eyes still hazed with desire, he lifted his dark head, a frown of puzzlement drawing his black brows together.

'What is it?'

'No!'

With a terrible, wrenching movement, the force of which took her across the lift to cannon into the opposite wall, Jenna pulled herself away from him.

'*No!*'

How could she have fallen prey to his calculated seduction? How could she have forgotten how easily he could switch on such passion, only to walk away when it no longer suited him? And how could she ever forget that such passion had led to the conception of their child, a baby that had died before it had ever seen the light of day? A baby that he had never ever asked about nor even acknowledged its existence?

'Hell and damnation, woman! What on earth's got into you?'

The lazy ease with which Connor got to his feet was the final insult, the ultimate destruction of what little remained of her self-esteem. That and the casually composed manner in which he smoothed down his clothing, combed a hand through the ruffled darkness of his hair. He might as well have just got up from a seat at a desk, or the dining table, not just abandoned a wild, impassioned lovemaking session—on the floor of a lift!

While she, by contrast, looked as if she'd been dragged very roughly through several hedges backwards. All around her in the mirrored walls of the lift compartment she could see her own reflection, repeated over and over again until it blurred together like some nightmarish kaleidoscope.

Jenna took one frantic look, then gulped painfully, her gaze skittering away again in panic. She couldn't bear the spectacle she made. Her hair was wildly tangled, falling in disorder around her flushed face. Her eyes were still glazed, the pupils dilated so that they were black, shocked pools above the hectic colour in her cheeks. And her clothes... She shuddered in horror at the sight.

The blue linen dress was somewhere up around her hips, exposing the tops of her stockings and the suspenders holding them in place. Its bodice was still unbuttoned, gaping widely over the swell of her breasts. The dainty scraps of silver-grey silk and lace that had been her bra were wrenched aside, exposing her nipples, and the skin around them was still reddened and marked by the evidence of Connor's passionate assault.

Acid burned in her stomach, nausea making her want to heave, and the sense of humiliation was made all the more unbearable by the coolly assessing way in which Connor was regarding her. She might only have been some particularly nasty specimen on a laboratory slab for all the concern he showed.

'Just what the hell is your problem, Jenna?'

'The problem is that you exist!' she flung at him, desperately pulling the front of her dress together over her reddened skin. 'That I was ever fool enough to be alone with you! That— Oh!'

It was a cry of despair as one of the buttons her flurried

fingers were trying to force back into its fastening snapped off and spun away somewhere on the opposite side of the lift. She couldn't cover herself quickly enough in order to hide her body and her shame from those fiendishly cold eyes, but the knowledge that he was watching her made it impossible to function with any degree of efficiency.

'Jenna—' Connor began, biting back his impatience with evident effort.

But Jenna couldn't listen to anything he said. She couldn't look at him, couldn't bear to be in the same place as he was. The minute that her appearance was restored to some degree of decorum, she crossed to the emergency phone and snatched up the receiver.

'I have to get out of here! I can't stay cooped up like this any longer!'

Panic swelled up inside her, blocking her throat, when there was nothing but silence at the other end of the phone.

'Why aren't they doing something?' she cried, her voice rising in hysteria. 'Where...?'

The words faded, died on a sensation of pure horror as, with a savage curse, Connor moved forward quickly and rammed his finger onto a button on the control panel. Immediately the lift whirred into life, jolted slightly, and began its descent once more.

'What...?'

She stared blankly, blinking in stunned confusion. But then, as the mists that clouded her head cleared, the truth dawned, and with it came the feeling of being trapped in an appalling nightmare. Only this was no dream, and she was hatefully wide awake, with no hope of the dawn ever bringing her a chance of escape.

'You—*you* did it!' She spat the words into his unyielding face, rage and hatred boiling over once and for all. 'You bastard! It was you all the time!'

He didn't even make a pretence of denying it, but simply inclined his head in agreement. The acknowledgement was so unemotional, so unapologetic, with no trace of shame

on his hard-boned features, that she came perilously close
to launching herself at him, fists flying. Only the realisation
that the lift was slowing once more, finally reaching the
ground floor, held her back from venting the violence of
her feelings in a very physical manner.

As soon as the doors opened she dashed towards the exit,
reassured by the sight of the empty foyer beyond. Even
though the mirrors all around told her that she had managed
to restore enough order to her appearance to survive all but
the closest scrutiny, she dreaded meeting anyone she knew
before she reached her mother's car.

But— 'Jenna!' Connor said sharply, and her headlong
flight was arrested as he reached out, his hand closing
tightly over her arm, pulling her back.

'Let go of me!' she demanded furiously. 'Let me out of
here!'

'When I've said all I want to.'

'All *you* want to!' Her laugh was high-pitched and
brittle. 'It seems to me you've said and done more than
enough already! I certainly don't want to hear a single word
you have to say.'

'You need to see that it isn't over between us. That
there's still—'

'It *is* over! How can I make you see that? Connor, there
is *nothing* between us now, nor will there ever be again.
And besides...'

In desperation she clutched at every straw she could find.
'You're forgetting about Saturday again.'

Wrenching her arm free from his grasp, she flung her
hand up between them, fingers splayed out in just the same
way as he had held it only a short time earlier.

'I may not have a ring to flaunt in your face, but I *am*
telling you to go to hell. Telling you to get out of my life
and never come back— Don't do that!' she cried as Connor
shook his dark head slowly, implacable rejection of her
words stamped into every hard line of his face. 'You're
forgetting about the wedding.'

Connor's smile almost destroyed her. It was cruel, malevolent, fiendish in its dark triumph.

'I'm forgetting nothing,' he told her with malign softness. 'You're not married yet. The wedding isn't until Saturday. That gives me another five days to prove to you that marrying this Graham will be the worst mistake you ever made in your life. I reckon that should be more than long enough.'

CHAPTER FOUR

'It's another parcel. *Another* wedding present!'

'Oh, not more!'

Jenna rolled her eyes in mock despair towards where her sister stood in the lounge doorway, having just returned from answering the summons of the front doorbell.

'Where on earth are we going to put them all, Susie? Who's it from this time?'

'From...' Susie peered at the return address on the outer wrapping. 'Mary and Charles—the Abbotts. You'd better put their names down on the list.'

'Yet more thank-you letters to write.' Jenna hunted under the piles of cards, wrapping paper and opened envelopes that already cluttered the large dark green settee, pulling out a rather battered spiral-bound notebook with a cry of triumph. 'This job seems to be going on for ever,' she added, scribbling down the new names at the end of an already lengthy list.

'I do think it's most unfair that all the etiquette books put it down as one of the bride's duties,' her sister commented, carefully balancing the parcel on a large pile of others of different shapes and sizes collected on the huge oak sideboard at the far end of the room. 'After all, they're presents for Graham too, but he gets all the pleasure of opening them and none of the drudgery of writing to everyone.'

'I shall tell him to do his share tonight,' Jenna laughed. 'He can find some way of expressing gratitude for yet another toaster...'

'Oh, don't!'

Susie gave a shudder at the thought of the three such

items that had already arrived at the Kenyon house in the past week.

'I rather suspect that *that*...' she nodded towards the most recently arrived parcel '...could be another one.'

'Susie—no! Please tell me you're kidding!'

'Felt the right size for a toaster to me. And you know that sort of rattle they make if you shake them...'

Jenna gave a groan and buried her face in her hands. Their shared laughter was interrupted by the sound of the bell ringing once more.

'Now who could this be? Not another delivery, surely.'

'I'll go; it's my turn,' Jenna said, getting to her feet and picking her way carefully through the litter of opened parcels, swatches of fabric and samples of lace that littered the floor. 'It gets more like a minefield in here every day,' she tossed over her shoulder on her way out into the hall. 'I shall be glad when Saturday's over. Why do weddings always create such chaos?'

'Well, it would be a lot easier if you weren't moving into a new flat at the same time.'

'Tell me about it! Marriages and house-moves just do not mix.' Jenna laughed as she pulled open the door.

The smile froze on her face, stiffening into the rigidity of disbelief as her eyes met those of the man on the doorstep. For a split second she considered slamming the door shut and telling her sister that the caller had been a double-glazing salesman, but the resigned conviction that such a tactic wouldn't work stilled her hand.

Connor would not just give up and go away politely. If she didn't face him now he would simply stay, probably with his finger firmly on the bell, until she was forced to acknowledge him.

'Hello, Connor,' she greeted coolly, praying he wouldn't be able to guess at the way her heart was tap-dancing inside her chest, making her breath catch painfully in her throat. 'What do you want?'

Connor's smile was brilliant, devastating in its effect on her peace of mind.

'To give you these.'

For a second Jenna could only stare in blank confusion at the bouquet of flowers he held out. Then, reacting purely automatically, her hands went out to take them.

'They're gorgeous! Orchids, no less!'

'Beautiful flowers for a beautiful bride.'

Something in that *'bride'* had a barbed hook that caught on her nerves and tugged painfully. Looking into his face, Jenna suddenly felt a sensation like the slow, insidious creeping of a dank, miserable fog slide into her mind, tainting her pleasure in the spectacular bouquet.

She'd got it all wrong. Foolishly, naively, seeing him here like this, she had assumed that he had come to apologise. That the flowers were to make amends for his behaviour in the lift the previous day. And in that spirit she had felt able to accept his gift.

But Connor was clearly totally unrepentant; saying he was sorry was obviously the last thing on his mind. His next words confirmed as much.

'I hoped you might reconsider your decision about having dinner with me.'

The nerve of the man! Was he incapable of taking no for an answer? How she regretted taking the flowers from him. In fact, she was strongly tempted to fling them right back in his face now that she saw his actions for what they really were.

This was just a new approach, a deliberate, calculated change of tack. Coming on strong—the caveman approach of the previous day—hadn't worked, so now he was trying another tactic.

As ominous and disturbing as the sound of a tolling church bell, the last words she had heard from him came back to haunt her.

'You're not married yet... That gives me another five days... I reckon that should be more than long enough.'

And before that, even more menacing and portentous: 'I do as I want now, and no one—*no one*—gets in my way.'

'I've not reconsidered anything. Nor do I intend to—at least, not anything to do with you.'

'Really? Don't you think—?'

'Jen, who is it?'

Susie's voice, softly curious, interrupted Connor's response, bringing his blue eyes swinging round to where she stood in the sitting-room doorway. With her long honey-coloured hair tumbling loose around her shoulders, and not a scrap of make-up on her delicate skin, Susie looked little more than a child, and years away from the just twenty that was her actual age. She also looked disturbingly like Jenna herself at the same age, if one ignored the difference in their colouring. A fact that was clearly not lost on Connor as his eyes widened for a moment in shock.

'Is there a problem?'

'No problem, Sue,' Jenna hastened to reassure her. 'Connor was just leaving.'

On the contrary, Connor looked as if he was fully deter-mined to stay put. And now he switched on his most bril-liant smile, turning it in Susie's direction.

'Hi, Susie,' he greeted casually. 'You've done some growing up since I last saw you.'

'Who…?' Susie moved until the man at the door was in range of her rather shortsighted vision. 'Connor Harding! Where did you spring from?'

'Business brought me back to Greenford, and I thought I'd renew the acquaintance of a few old friends.'

'And of course my sister was the first on your list. Did you bring those flowers? They're gorgeous!'

Silently Jenna cursed the nosiness that had brought Susie out into the hall before she had been able to get rid of Connor. Almost six years younger than Jenna herself, her sister had been little more than a child at the time of the devastating events that had shattered her world.

With her parents away on the other side of the world,

visiting an aunt and uncle in Australia, and Susie on a school exchange in France, Grant, her eldest brother, had taken charge. He had insisted that the full, miserable details of what had happened, should remain a secret between them, and, already emotionally devastated, mentally at rock-bottom, Jenna had been only too glad to hide away the sordid details from as many people as she could.

But now, seeing the immediate effect that megawatt smile had on her susceptible sibling, she could have wished that Susie was a little more in the know about just what sort of a man Connor Harding was.

'They're—'

'Connor can't stop,' Jenna inserted sharply, suddenly very much afraid that he would repeat his 'beautiful flowers for a beautiful bride' remark. 'He has an important meeting to go to,' she improvised hastily.

'Oh, that's a pity. I was just about to make a pot of tea, and I thought you might like a cup.'

'That would be most welcome.'

Connor blithely ignored the furious glare she shot him, warning him silently on no account to accept.

'It really is very hot, and I could do with a drink.'

'But…'

'And don't worry about that meeting, Jenna,' he continued with an infuriatingly false reassuring smile. 'I should have told you; it's been postponed until tomorrow.'

'I'll put the kettle on, then.'

Susie drifted off towards the kitchen, pausing to frown her confusion when Jenna, finding herself quite unable to tolerate the thought of letting this man into the house, remained where she was, blocking the doorway.

'Jen?' she questioned, with just enough suspicion shading her voice to have her sister starting like a nervous cat as she swung away from the door.

'I'll make the tea,' she said, painfully aware of the way the shake in her voice betrayed the whirling turmoil of her thoughts. 'And I'd better put these flowers in water.'

Put them straight in the dustbin, more likely, she added inwardly, ignoring the pang of regret that twisted inside her at the thought of all that bright beauty in amongst the potato peelings and the discarded packaging. It wasn't the flowers' fault that they were tainted by having come from Connor Harding.

'Leave that to me.' Susie forestalled her by turning and taking the bouquet from her. 'You and Connor have a lot of catching up to do. If I remember rightly, you were once very close to being an item.'

'Hardly that!' Jenna protested as the kitchen door swung to behind her sister. Knowing she had no possible alternative, she stepped back to allow Connor entry into the wide hallway. 'I suppose you'd better come in,' was all she could manage, through gritted teeth.

'How could I refuse such a very gracious invitation?' he returned, with a sardonic mockery that grated over her already tightly stretched nerves like rough sandpaper.

His smile held no warmth at all. On the contrary, it was cold and disagreeable, shaded with worrying hints of dangers she could only guess at. And his eyes were equally glacial, all emotion blanked off.

'Do you realise,' Connor went on in the same tone when they were back in the sitting room, 'that this is the first time I have actually set foot in the hallowed surroundings of the Kenyon mansion?'

Pausing in the act of clearing a small amount of the clutter from one of the armchairs—basic politeness decreed that at least she should let him sit down—Jenna could only nod silently. Such meetings as they had managed had always taken place well away from this house—in some anonymous pub, sometimes at the tennis club, or on rare, apocalyptic occasions—hot colour washed over her skin at the thought—in the house he had bought his mother.

'And nothing dreadful has happened. No trumpets of doom sounding, or walls crumbling in shock. But I'd be willing to bet that old Grandad Abel will be spinning around in his grave in horror. And your eldest brother and self-appointed bodyguard will be far from delighted when he knows.'

'Grant no longer lives here.'

She felt shaken and strangely raw, as if that mocking tongue had the ability to flay the skin from her bones, layer by protective layer, exposing the vulnerable flesh beneath.

'All of my brothers have their own homes now.'

Homes and families, she recalled miserably. Even Joe, the youngest of the Kenyon sons, had recently become a father for the first time.

Her bright green gaze clouded in pain, bitter tears stinging at her eyes as she recalled how she had felt when, only six weeks before, she had gone to the hospital to see her newest nephew for the first time. Radiant with happiness, and totally unaware of the past, Meg, the baby's mother, had naturally urged her to lift the precious bundle from the cot and hold him.

Jenna's teeth dug into her lower lip now, as they had then, as she remembered how she had fought to hold back from weeping at the sensation of cuddling the tiny frame close. A terrible sense of loss had assailed her, even after all this time, the warmth, the clean, milky smell of his skin catching in her throat and threatening to choke her.

'And soon you will have, too... A home of your own,' Connor supplied in explanation when, still struggling with the pain of her memories, she could only frown her lack of understanding. 'With the so-nice Graham.'

'I already have a flat of my own—and a business—in London!' Jenna reminded him sharply.

Too sharply, she realised, seeing the frown that crossed his autocratic features. Even in his youth Connor had never suffered fools gladly, and obviously the man he had become was much less prepared to tolerate anything he considered even remotely impertinent.

But she had to get the conversation away from the potentially explosive subject of Graham and the wedding before Susie came back with the tea. To her intense relief, Connor seemed prepared to follow her lead.

'You never did tell me what you actually do,' he said, with an ease that belied the disturbing tension in the firm jaw.

He lowered himself into the seat she had cleared as he spoke, stretching his long legs out in front of him and leaning back his dark head to look up at her, eyes narrowing assessingly.

'What career did you decide on in the end?'

'I—organise things.' Hunting for somewhere to stack the papers she had removed from his chair, Jenna was grateful for an excuse to avoid that cold-eyed scrutiny. 'Parties— birthdays, coming of age, engagements, anniversaries—that sort of thing.'

'And is the venture successful?' To her surprise he sounded genuinely interested.

'I do all right. Nothing in your sort of sphere, of course. Financially, Celebrations is strictly small fry, but I make a comfortable living.'

'And will you keep your job once you're married?'

'Of course! I haven't spent five years building up a reputation simply to throw it all in once I have a ring on my finger.'

'Won't it be a little tricky running a business based in London when Graham is—as you so proudly told me—all set for a wonderful promotion up here?'

Inwardly, Jenna flinched as if she'd been stung. The less contentious topic of conversation had turned out to be anything but. Somehow they were back in the potential minefield of Graham and the wedding, and if she wasn't extremely careful everything was going to blow up, right in her face.

'There is a very efficient inter-city service between here and the capital, you know!' she returned tartly. 'Though I suppose those of us who spend our lives being chauffeured around in limos can't be expected to know that! And

Celebrations isn't a one-woman show. The comfortable living means I earn enough to pay two assistants. One full-time, and another who comes in mornings or afternoons each week—more if things are really busy.'

What had put that expression on his face? The faintly amused smile that curled the corners of his wide mouth tugged at her nerves, making her shift uncomfortably from one foot to another. Was she protesting too much? Stating her case rather too strongly and emphatically?

'Either of them would be perfectly capable of running things on a day-to-day basis if I couldn't get in,' she finished uneasily.

'So you've got it all under control... Are you ever going to sit down?' A hint of exasperation escaped his careful restraint. 'You must have moved that pile of papers to six different places already! It's making me dizzy just to watch you.'

'Sorry!' She hadn't realised just how much of her inner nervousness she was giving away. 'They're name-cards, actually—for the seating arrangements. They just came back from the printer's. We were checking them when you arrived. They're—'

'Damn you, Jenna!' Connor finally lost his grip on the temper he had been reining in with an effort. 'I'm not interested in name-cards, or any other details of your wonderful wedding to the bank manager of the year! That isn't why I came here, and you know it!'

'Then why are you here?'

Silly question. Very silly. After all, she knew exactly what the answer would be. And, in spite of her resolve not to, she had given him the perfect opportunity to rake it all up once again.

'Don't play games, Jenna! You know—I came to ask you to have dinner with me tonight, and I don't intend to leave this house until you say yes.'

'But why are you so set on this?'

She'd seen the contempt in his eyes, the way it was

stamped into every hard bone in his face. She couldn't understand how he could feel such scorn for her and still want to spend time in her company.

Except, of course, that her foolish weakness in the lift the day before had given him hope of an easy conquest. Was he such a sexual opportunist that he was prepared to ignore the way he felt mentally if the result was a brief physical satisfaction?

'I told you how I felt yesterday!'

'And I told you I didn't believe it!'

Putting both his hands on the dark green velvet-covered arms of the chair, he pushed himself upright, coming towards her before she had time to realise what was happening and catching hold of her shoulders, hard fingers clamping over delicate bone when she would have spun away.

'Nothing you said convinced me that this tepid "fondness" you have for your bank manager holds one tenth of the fire, the passion, the sheer mind-blowing hunger we once shared. And could still share again.'

'No...'

Jenna tried to turn her face away, but found it impossible. She was caught and held by the mesmeric intensity of his voice, the dangerous light in his eyes.

'It's still there, Jenny Wren; surely you can feel it! It's all around us, like the build-up of static before a storm, and it must be acknowledged or it will tear you apart. You're rejecting part of yourself if you deny it, and you'll never be able to live with the consequences if you do.'

'No...' Jenna tried again, with no more success.

'Think about how you'll feel when you wake up after— what?—a year?—less?—of marriage to your Graham. When you realise that he doesn't satisfy you, that he leaves you hungry where he should feed you. What will you do...?'

'I said *no!*'

With a strength she hadn't known she possessed, Jenna wrenched herself free of his grasp, the force of her action taking her halfway across the room.

'I won't have dinner with you! I don't *want* to have dinner with you! You can argue till you're blue in the face and you won't change the way I feel. So why won't you take no for an answer?'

After the dark eloquence of his argument just moments before, Connor's sudden silence was strangely shocking. For a second his head went back, deep blue eyes looking stunned, as if she had actually physically slapped him hard. But then just as swiftly he regained control, and was back on the attack.

'Because—because I *can't*, damn you!'

She had been wrong in the idea of an attack, Jenna thought dazedly. His answer had sounded as if it had been forced from him, as if he would rather have said *anything* but that.

'Because I can't do anything else! Because after seeing you again I find myself feeling as if I'm twenty-six again, wanting you so much that I can't think, can't eat, can't exist if you're not mine! And I always knew that was how it would be, in spite of everything that's happened! It's as inevitable as the fact that the sun will set tonight and rise again tomorrow morning—that the morning after will always follow the night before.'

Shaking his dark head roughly, as if in despair at himself, he swung away from her and stared out at the sunlit garden, shoulders hunched and hands pushed deep into the pockets of his jeans.

'Because I can't help myself. And no matter how hard I fight it, no matter how much I twist and turn in order to break free, no matter what force I use to try and drive it from my mind, it's always there—*you're* always there.'

With a suddenness that had her taking a step backwards he whirled round again, and what she read in his face had her mouth opening on a gasp of shock.

This was how he had looked in those first few moments when they had come face to face in the foyer of the hotel—was it only the day before yesterday? This blazing scorn, mixed explosively with savage loathing, had been there in that first burning look that had swept over her. It had felt like such a brutal assault that she had almost believed the force of it should have shrivelled her where she stood, leaving nothing but a pile of ashes on the tiled floor.

And it had stayed all through their encounter yesterday. It might have been buried under the dark sensuality of his words and actions, but it had been there, even when he'd held her in his arms, when he had kissed her, caressed her, made love to her.

'I don't want to feel like this any more than you do...'

Connor's voice was thick and rough, making Jenna shiver in horror at the thought of the way those kisses and caresses had been mixed with this searing contempt that now burned at her skin, eating away inside her like acid. Because he had no right to any such feeling. If anyone felt that way it should be her, after the appalling way he had treated her, the cruelty of his desertion when she had needed him most.

Even worse was the obvious self-disgust that he didn't even try to hide. He wanted her—couldn't help it, couldn't stop himself from experiencing the blazing desire he had described so eloquently. But he didn't like feeling that way. He hated the thought of being unable to control that hunger, no matter how much he wanted to.

How dared he? Jenna's fury was like a red haze before her eyes, blinding her to everything but the feelings boiling up inside her. How *dare* he despise her when he was the one who had behaved with such callous brutality, just the memory of which still had the power to rip into her heart and leave it bleeding and raw all over again.

'I can only give in to it, and hope that by indulging it totally, by giving myself up to it, I'll be able to work it out of my system.'

'Some kind of aversion therapy, you mean?' Jenna's tone was corrosive.

'If you like,' was the reply, with a shockingly careless shrug of those broad shoulders.

'But *why*? What have I done to make you hate me so much?'

'You—'

'Tea's served!'

The sound of Susie's bright, cheerful voice made Connor clamp his mouth shut on what he had been about to say.

'Martha's baked one of her amazing chocolate cakes, so I brought that along as well.' Blithely unaware of the dangerous emotional currents swirling round the room, Susie deposited a laden tray on the nearest empty space. 'I hope you're hungry.'

Jenna managed an incoherent murmur that might have been agreement, but Connor didn't even turn his eyes in her sister's direction. Instead, he directed their cold, compelling force straight at Jenna's flushed, angry face as he completed his interrupted sentence.

'You're a Kenyon,' he tossed at her. 'Isn't that enough?'

Of course it wasn't enough! Not anything like enough!

Like her, Connor had never subscribed to the supposed feud. He had laughed at her concern about it, only letting it get to him when she had let her fear rule their meetings, curtailing their freedom to be together. Or when one of her brothers had done something particularly unpleasant. When he had broken her heart it had been for far more selfish reasons than because of a need to get at her family through her.

'What do you mean, she's a Kenyon?' Susie asked, frowning prettily. 'Oh, don't tell me—you're not reviving that old nonsense, are you? I thought you two were way above that sort of thing. After all, it's ancient history.'

Right now, it felt like very *recent* history, Jenna reflected wretchedly. The pain of Connor's betrayal was as fresh and stark as if it had been inflicted the day before. She could only be grateful that all those years ago Susie had been away, and so she had missed the whole, terrible drama. She had never even known of the emergency rush to hospital, the bleak despair of the days that had followed, the struggle Jenna had had to hide the truth from her.

And when Susie had come back to Greenford Connor had gone, leaving the town for good. His father had died some years before, and he had taken his mother to live with him, setting her up in luxury in the palatial country house that was his home.

She hadn't gone through all that then, in order to keep the whole sorry story a secret, only to have it raked up again now, when she had finally begun to feel that she could hope to put it all behind her.

So now she switched on an over-bright smile that she prayed didn't look as blatantly false to Susie as it felt to her.

'Connor's just feeling peeved,' she said, with what she hoped was airy insouciance. 'He asked me out to dinner and I said no...'

'You said *no*!' Susie echoed in disbelief. 'Jenna, you can't be serious! You...'

'I don't have time,' Jenna jumped in hastily, terrified at the thought of what her sister might reveal. 'There's so much to do before the wedding, and besides, it wouldn't be appropriate...'

'Not appropriate?' Connor inserted dryly, his tone making it plain just how little he thought of that excuse. 'What could anyone find to object to in two old friends having dinner together?'

Jenna rolled her eyes in exasperation at the words he had used. Anything less like 'old friends' than herself and this monster of a man would be hard to find.

'Connor's right, Jen! You should reconsider your decision,' Susie urged. 'Dinner would be fun.'

Fun was the last thing it would be. If Susie had only heard the things Connor had said just moments before she came back into the room, then she would know exactly why her sister would rather contemplate spending her evening in a pit of poisonous snakes than with the man before her.

Her already whirling emotions were only aggravated by the faintly smug smile at the corner of his lips, the glint of triumph in his eyes. He really believed that all he had to do was stand back and let Susie do the persuading for him. Well, he very definitely had another think coming!

'And you know you never got over that crush you had on Connor all those years ago—not really!' her sister teased, cutting across the sound of strangled protest that was all Jenna could manage.

'*Sue!*' she hissed through clenched teeth, but was totally ignored.

'Do you know,' Susie went on confidingly to Connor, who had now folded his arms across his broad chest and was leaning back against the wall, watching the scene before him with every sign of amused enjoyment, 'Jenna must have been your most ardent fan imaginable in the days when you were playing at Wimbledon. She was glued to every match.'

'I was glued to *any* match!' Jenna inserted desperately. 'It didn't matter who was playing. You know I always loved tennis.' It was, after all, the thing that had brought them together in the first place all those years ago, when she had been little more than a girl.

'You *watched* any match,' Susie retorted. 'But you always used to shout Connor on, cheering and clapping if he won.'

To Jenna's extreme discomfort, Connor's dark eyes were now fastened on her face, and the scarred brow lifted in sardonic enquiry when she turned a harassed and indignant glance in his direction.

'I always appreciated skill and talent, and no one could deny you had more than your share of both!' she flung at him defiantly, challenging him to make more of that than was actually there.

'I'm flattered,' Connor drawled, sounding anything but.

He had never been short on self-esteem, and he was only too well aware of the fact that as a tennis player he had deserved any praise that had been heaped on him. It was his behaviour as a human being that was a very different matter.

'So won't you at least give me a chance to thank—belatedly, I admit—my most ardent fan for those years of loyal support?'

Not again! Did the man never give up? He must have a hide thicker than that of a rhinoceros if he could still persist in spite of her obvious unwillingness to accept his invitation.

'I told you, I don't *want*—'

'Oh, Jen, it's only a meal!' Susie put in, unconsciously echoing Connor's argument of the day before. 'Had you decided where to go, Connor?'

'Well, I had thought the Voltaire.'

'Then you are quite definitely out of your mind, sister mine! You can't turn down dinner at the Voltaire. The food there is *amazing*. I'd sell my soul to a man who'd treat me to it.'

Connor's smile grew, darkened, and Jenna felt her heart miss a beat. She knew what was coming. It was stamped on his face as clearly as if she could read his mind.

'Then perhaps I'd do better to take your sister after all, Jenna. It seems she'd be more appreciative of the offer, and—'

'No!'

She couldn't let him continue. This was even worse than she had thought. She had seen the look on his face when he had realised just how much her baby sister had grown up in the time he'd been away. She would rather die than expose Susie to this man's predatory charms. It would be like leaving an innocent lamb in the care of a hungry tiger.

And as to what her sister might confide in him over a bottle of wine, she couldn't even bear to think.

'No?' Connor questioned softly, the mocking gleam in

his eyes brightening, becoming positively fiendish in its triumph. 'Changed your mind, Jenny Wren?'

'All right!' She had to force it from between clenched teeth, even now wishing there was some way she could hold it back, but knowing there was no escape.

He had out-manoeuvred her brilliantly, and he knew it. She was trapped, with no way out, no alternative but to say yes. She couldn't bear to look into his dark face, to see the gloating satisfaction that must be etched there, the amusement at her discomfiture.

'All right, I'll have dinner with you. But only dinner, is that clear? *Nothing* else!'

'Dinner's all I asked for,' Connor assured her smoothly. 'There's no hidden agenda.'

And if she could believe that, Jenna told herself in the privacy of her thoughts, how much easier life would be. But with Connor there was always a hidden agenda, and that was a prospect that made her heart quail in fearful anticipation of just what might be ahead of her.

CHAPTER FIVE

TONIGHT was a first, Jenna realised with something of a shock as she swept a brush through the dark silk of her hair in the last of her preparations for the evening ahead of her. The first time she and Connor had ever had dinner together in a restaurant. The first time they had ever been out in public in the town of Greenford.

It had all been so very different all those years ago. Then, they had met as secretly as possible, and usually miles away from her home town. That had been at her insistence. Although she had started out regarding the Kenyon-Harding feud as simply laughable, the height of adult nonsense, growing maturity had brought a healthy respect for the force of feeling it engendered in her father and, through his influence, in her older brothers.

She had come to realise that the problems which had their roots in the events of so many years before, and which succeeding generations had managed to complicate even further, could not be unravelled as easily as she had once hoped. And so she had chosen discretion above the dubious appeal of rebellion, deciding that what her family didn't know wouldn't hurt them.

And besides, she had wanted to consider Connor more than anyone. As the last surviving male member of the Harding family, he had always borne the brunt of her family's hostility while she was growing up. If her brothers, and most particularly the eldest, Grant, discovered he was seeing her, the results could be disastrous. More so for Connor than for her.

Connor.

'Damn you, Connor!'

Jenna tossed down the hairbrush and stared into the mirror. Her eyes showed more of the truth than she cared to acknowledge. Dark and deep as a mossy pool, they were shadowed by the recollection of the past, the memory of how it had once been and the loss of so much innocent happiness.

'*Damn* you, Connor!' she cried again reproachfully. 'Damn you for proving them all right!'

Connor Harding had always been a part of her life. 'That Harding boy' was the way her father had always referred to him, usually in the most derogatory of tones, while Grant, Will and Joe simply spoke of 'Harding', nothing more, spitting the name out like a violent curse.

Jenna herself had simply been intrigued. She had watched Connor from the distance the five-year difference in their ages automatically created, curious to discover what the focus of so much anger and hatred might be like.

What she had seen was a tall, dark youth with brilliant blue eyes, a face that even in the awkward years of early adolescence clearly revealed the promise of the stunningly attractive man he would grow to be, and a lithe, muscular frame that already towered above most of his classmates and contemporaries. Connor Harding was quite simply a hunk, in the opinion of all the girls at the local school. Not only that, but he was intelligent, often carrying off year prizes and other awards, and he was simply brilliant at sports, particularly tennis.

It was tennis that had first brought them together. Tennis and—in a way that was eventually to form something of a pattern—Grant's bullying behaviour. Because Jenna had soon learned that the antipathy between her brothers and Connor Harding was of their making, not his.

Any fights that broke out they started, though that was not how it was reported at home, of course. And Grant was usually the prime instigator. It was Grant who had caused the problem that had brought her to Connor's notice that first time.

It had been summer, the day of the annual sports and tennis tournament. Of the result of the latter there had been very little doubt. Only the week before, at barely seventeen, Connor Harding had won the County Championships for the second time, and everyone knew that, barring a catastrophe, he would walk away with the school trophy as well. But then disaster had struck, and by chance Jenna had been there when Connor discovered it.

Like all the rest of her year, she had been heading out to the sports field to watch the afternoon's activities when she had realised that she had left her watch behind in her coat pocket. As it was a brand-new twelfth birthday present, the fear of losing it had been overwhelming, and she had dashed back to find it. Anxious to rejoin her friends, she had hurried along, not really looking where she was going, attention concentrated on fastening the strap around her wrist, and so had blundered into an unexpected obstacle in the middle of what she'd thought was a deserted corridor.

'Hey, steady!'

At first, with her hair over her face, temporarily blinding her, she didn't realise who held her. But a moment later, sweeping the tangled locks back and away from her eyes, she looked up into the strongly carved face of Connor Harding, and felt a hot wash of blood creep over her skin in embarrassment.

'I'm sorry— I— Thank you, but I can stand now. You can let me go.'

'Sure?' He sounded as if he doubted her word, but he let her go just the same, seeming to dismiss her from his thoughts as his attention switched back to whatever had held it in the first place.

'I...' Jenna began, but then all coherent thought was wiped from her mind, swept away on a tide of pure horror as her blurred gaze cleared and focused on what he held in his hands.

The tennis racquet was one of the very best that money could buy. She recognised that because both Grant and Will had one, and she knew exactly how much they cost. And it was clearly almost brand-new. But it had been treated appallingly—the handle shattered, strings cut. It was damaged beyond repair.

'Oh, *no!*' It was a cry of shock and distress. 'Did I do that?' Had she stood on it by accident, trampled it in her headlong flight? 'Oh, Connor, I didn't mean...'

'It's all right,' he hastened to reassure her. 'You didn't have anything to do with it.'

But then those vivid eyes had looked into her face, Connor apparently seeing her clearly for the first time, and his expression had hardened worryingly.

'Or did you? You're the Kenyon kid, aren't you? Grant's sister?' His tone was definitely dangerous now.

'Are you saying Grant did *that*? Oh, no, Connor! He...'

'He?' Connor prompted hardly, when once more the words dried in her throat.

But Jenna couldn't answer him. Her thoughts were whirling frantically, recalling a conversation overheard the night before. Grant and Will talking about the tennis tournament and a comment she had only half understood.

'I'd give the world to knock that bastard off his perch for once,' Will had grumbled. 'If he was out of the running, I'd win that cup for sure.'

And Grant's voice answering, rich with a calculating triumph that, even not knowing what he meant, had made her shiver in uneasy reaction.

'Don't give up yet, little brother. There are ways and means...'

Now, looking down at the ruined racquet in Connor's strong, tanned hands, Jenna's throat dried painfully and she had to swallow hard before she could speak.

'I—I'm sorry,' she croaked. 'Don't you have another?'

'Another?' Connor's laughter was harsh, scraping over raw nerves. 'Another one like this? Do you know how hard I had to work in order to earn the cash for this one? We're not all made of money, like the Kenyons.'

'Oh…' It was a low, shocked whisper. 'Connor, I'm truly sorry, but it *is* only a school…'

Yet again her voice failed her as she saw him shake his dark head in cold rejection of her attempt at pacification, his wide mouth twisting bitterly.

'You don't know the half of it, kid. It may be only a school tournament, but it could have been so much more. Ron Beaumont—head of PE—just told me that he'd had a phone call from a tennis coach—an international coach— who'd heard I was good. He's going to be here this afternoon, to watch.'

'To watch you?' Jenna couldn't keep the excitement from her voice. 'Do you mean that he might decide to take you on, that you could have a chance of a professional career? Wimbledon and…' Once more her eyes went to the racquet in his hands. 'Oh, no!'

'Oh, yes,' Connor confirmed cynically. 'My big chance and your brother's ruined it.'

'No!' Jenna exclaimed as inspiration struck. 'I mean, no, he hasn't ruined it. Not yet!'

'Oh, sure. I suppose you just happen to have another…'

'No, I don't, but *Grant* does! He's got his own racquet, almost identical to that one! And I know for sure he won't be using it today because he's in the athletics team; he's not even taking part in the tennis tournament. If I could sneak out of school and dash home, I could… No?' She couldn't believe it when he shook his head.

'No,' he declared adamantly. 'No way. I can't let you do it. What if you were caught? If one of the staff saw you, or, worse, if Grant himself found out?'

'No one will see me if I go out the back way. And even if Grant did find out, I can handle him,' she declared, with more confidence than she actually felt. 'He may be a bit of a bully to others, but to me he's a pussycat! He's my big brother after all. Come on, Connor,' she cajoled, seeing from his expression that he was weakening. 'We can do it.'

'Well…'

'And just think...' Jenna pushed home her advantage with a wickedly gleeful smile. 'Beating Grant—both my brothers—at their own game, using his racquet to do it—and he'll never even know!'

She knew from his face that she'd convinced him, and before he'd had time to reconsider she was already on her way, dashing down the corridor at top speed, pausing only to toss a breathless, 'See you at the gate in ten minutes. Wimbledon, here you come!' back at him before she disappeared.

'Jenna!' Susie's voice reached her from the bottom of the stairs. 'Jen! Your date's here!'

'He's not my *date*!' Jenna yelled back in exasperation, before realisation dawned fully as she registered just what her sister had said.

Connor, *here*, now! That wasn't at all how things were supposed to go!

Snatching up her jacket and her bag, she clattered down the stairs in frantic haste, pulling up short at the sight of the tall, elegantly dressed figure who stood in the hall.

'I told you I'd meet you at the restaurant!' she flung at him furiously, managing to get the words out fairly evenly in spite of the way that her heart was thundering at three times its normal rate. And not just because of her headlong dash from her room.

The evening hadn't started yet, and already she felt well on her way to being tipsy, in spite of the fact that she hadn't touched a drop of anything alcoholic. The devastating combination of Connor's azure eyes, gleaming sable hair and powerfully athletic build was ruinous enough to her composure. But when that potent mixture was encased in the civilised trappings of an exquisitely tailored navy suit with a shirt in a softer blue that picked up the tones of his eyes, it was positively lethal to rational thought.

'I know what you said,' Connor returned with maddening calm. 'But that's not how it's going to be any more. I won't be hidden in some dark alleyway or smuggled into a meeting under cover of darkness. It's more than time this stupid feud was over and forgotten. Quite frankly, I seriously doubt that your father will have apoplexy at the sight of me.'

That was not at all the major worry that had filled Jenna's thoughts when Susie had warned her of Connor's arrival. But perhaps it was safer to let him think that way.

'No.' Jenna admitted. 'As a matter of fact you're probably right, although he's not here this evening. I realise now that I wasn't seeing things quite straight all those years ago. My father used to be so set against you only because of what he'd heard. He was told that you caused trouble for the Kenyons, that you started fights at school...'

'And no prizes for guessing who fed those stories to him.'

Eyes almost as dark a navy as the material of his suit clashed with her own cloudy green ones, and the bitter cynicism she read in their depths took her back to that very first meeting on the day of the school tennis tournament.

Connor had won the championship, of course. He had defeated every opponent put up against him, without even the loss of a single set in any match. And the professional coach who had come to watch had spotted his potential at once. That same afternoon he had offered to take on Connor's training and development as a tennis player, and barely twenty-four hours later they had left Greenford together. The next time Jenna had seen Connor Harding had been on the television, being trumpeted as one of the country's newest hopes to be the latest Wimbledon champion.

Grant had been furious. For days the whole family had been at the mercy of his black, violent moods. Jenna herself had only just managed to return the borrowed racquet to her brother's room without being found out, and she had shuddered to think what might have happened if he had ever suspected what she'd been up to.

'I think I see the hand of Big Brother at work in all this,'

Connor drawled now, his deeply sardonic tone making her start like a nervous cat with the disturbed realisation of just how close he had come to the direction of her own private thoughts. 'Wouldn't you agree, Jenny Wren?'

'I told you not to call me that!'

She pounced on the only thing she felt capable of handling right now, not liking the way his use of that old, mocking nickname seemed to reduce her once more to the awkward, gauche teenager she had once been.

It had been almost six years before Connor had been seen in Greenford again, and when he had come back he'd been trailing clouds of glory as a result of his success on the international tennis circuit. He had left as an adolescent, with no money and little experience of the world, and returned a fully-grown man, wealthy, sophisticated, and above all handsome beyond Jenna's wildest dreams.

'Why not?' Connor questioned, a gleam of mocking amusement in his eyes. 'I can think of nothing more apt for the way you looked at eighteen—all wild brown hair, bright eyes and skinny legs.'

'I'd just finished growing!' Jenna growled, scowling furiously both at him and the memory of the Jenna Kenyon he had found on his return to Greenford.

Her growing up had not been as kind to her as his had been to him. She had grown tall, but not feminine, the curves that would merit that accolade only coming later, so that she had often been teased about her overly slender, almost boyish figure. Her hair had been lighter then, a sort of nondescript mouse, and so fine that the slightest touch of wind or rain had turned it into a wild haze around her head. As a result she had been painfully shy, colouring desperately if anyone, particularly any member of the opposite sex, so much as spoke to her.

And Connor had capitalised mercilessly on that sensitivity. He had treated her with a lofty condescension, or suddenly switched to a teasing flirtation that had her blushing furiously and stumbling over her words, tongue-tied with embarrassment. So she had been stunned and disbelieving when he had asked her to meet him for a drink.

'M-Me?' she had stammered. 'You don't mean it! You can't...'

'Can't I, Jenny Wren? Believe me, I do mean it—every word.'

'But why me?'

'Perhaps I remember a long-ago meeting—a kid who came to my rescue like some unexpected guardian angel. A helper without whom my life could have been so very different.'

Bleak disappointment had twisted inside Jenna's vulnerable heart. She should have realised. Should have known that a sophisticated, successful, devastatingly handsome man like Connor wouldn't be attracted to a schoolgirl mouse of a creature like her. He only wanted to thank her, after all these years, for the way she had borrowed Grant's racquet for him.

But she'd gone all the same. After insisting that they go somewhere where no one else would see them, she had agreed to meet him and spent the rest of the hours between then and the time they had arranged in a state of such nervous excitement that it had been like a fever in her blood. She had changed her clothes over a dozen times, altered her make-up almost as often. And she had created a careful cover story to convince her parents that she was meeting up with friends who, like her, had just left the local sixth form college.

Jenna sighed deeply, remembering the naïve adolescent she had been then. If only she had listened, *really* listened when Connor had talked to her that night. If she had, she might have spared herself bitter heartbreak and desolation.

But she had been adrift on a sea of excitement, and almost delirious with happiness at being alone with this stunning man who had actually asked her out. She had even managed to convince herself that this was a date, not just the belated gesture of a man who felt indebted to someone he still regarded as the child he had met long ago. And so she hadn't really taken in exactly what he was saying when, in answer to an artless comment about how satisfied he must be with everything he had achieved since he had left Greenford, he had shaken his head firmly.

'Not *satisfied*, Jenny Wren, never that. Satisfaction is stagnation; you have to be hungry—to really want the success. If you're not, you'll never make it.'

'But surely now...'

'You think it's eased?' Connor had looked deep into her eyes, his own blue gaze dark and intent as it fixed on her bemused green one. 'Sweetheart, I'm only twenty-three. There's so much more I want to achieve. Of course I'm still hungry. If anything, it's stronger than ever before. In this game you can't afford to stand still. And there's no room for Mr Nice Guy. It's a jungle, kill or be killed, and I don't intend to let anything stand in my way.'

'Why the big sigh?' Connor asked now, having caught her unthinking response to her thoughts. 'Are you still piqued at that nickname?'

The hint of amusement in his voice clashed so badly with the bitterness of her memories that all she could so was silently shake her head, sending the dark silk of her hair flying.

'Hey!'

Reaching out, he caught her face in gentle hands, stilling the nervous movement, forcing her to look him straight in the face.

'You know it doesn't fit any more,' he told her softly, the warm honey of his voice flowing smoothly over her disordered senses. His darkened gaze slid down over her slender frame in the burgundy silk softly-tailored trouser suit, worn with a black lace tee-shirt underneath. 'You know you grew into a glorious bird of paradise.'

Gentle fingers slid through her hair, sweeping it back from her face before the carefully controlled power of those strong hands smoothed over the delicate skin of her cheeks, following the line of her cheekbones. Completely mesmerised, Jenna could only stare in wide-eyed confusion, unable to frame a single word.

'You're a beautiful woman, Jenna. Stunning.' That soft voice had deepened, grown husky with a new and disturbing intensity. 'And it seems to me that you've grown more beautiful with every year that's passed. When I first met you, you were just a cute kid, but any fool with eyes in his head could see the potential there. See the beauty that was all there, just waiting to develop.'

Jenna's tongue flickered out, moistened desperately dry lips, and her heart kicked sharply against her ribs as she saw his brilliant gaze drop to follow the tiny movement.

'You...' she tried, but was unable to complete the sentence.

Connor's laugh was low and sensual.

'I knew. Why do you think I came back that second time—when you were twenty-one?'

And now she knew for sure that he was lying! He hadn't come back for her at all.

'You were forced into taking a break as a result of injury.'

A broken ankle had shattered his chances at the French Open that year, putting the prospect of Wimbledon very much in doubt, and as a result he had come back to Greenford to convalesce, ending up as bored and restless as a caged tiger after a couple of weeks in his mother's house.

Bitterly Jenna cursed the cruel twist of fate that had brought her home at just the same time. She had been away at college, but with her course finished had been killing time while she waited for the results of various job applications. With their Australian trip coming up, her parents had been glad to have her at home to look after the house and Susie, before she left for France.

'I don't flatter myself it had anything to do with me!'

With a violent movement she wrenched her face away

from his caressing hands, brutally ignoring the pained protest from her bewitched senses at the loss of the delight his
touch had induced.

'Now, are we going for this meal or not? I may have
been blackmailed into this, but I'd prefer it to be over and
done with as quickly as possible.'

'Your wish is my command!' Connor growled, sketching
a mockery of a salute that had nothing of the deferential in
it but was as insolent as a slap in the face. 'My car is
outside.'

The short trip to the restaurant was completed in a hostile, uncomfortable silence, only the noticeable sharpness
about Connor's movements, each change of gear or touch
of his hands on the wheel, revealing the simmering temper
he was barely managing to keep in check.

At his side, Jenna sat stiffly tense in her seat. She had
been dreading this evening from the start, and now it
seemed that it was going to be far worse than she could
ever have anticipated. How had she got herself into this?
Surely nothing on earth could make the situation any worse.

She was wrong. As Connor parked the car just a few
yards from the entrance to Voltaire's, a tall figure on the
opposite side of the road caught her eye. As she recognised
him Jenna's heart jerked violently, then plummeted down
to somewhere beneath the soles of her elegant patent leather
shoes with a speed that made her head reel.

Dear God, no! she prayed silently. Let this not be happening!

But her desperate entreaty went unheeded. Because in
that moment the man across the road looked directly at
Connor's car, and at Jenna herself sitting in the front seat.
Immediately a wide grin spread across his face and his hand
came up in an exuberant gesture of greeting.

'It seems that someone wants your attention.' Connor's
tone was scathingly sardonic. 'Do you know him?'

Jenna's throat seemed to have seized up, paralysing her
vocal cords. She could only nod silently, fighting against

the urge to shudder in horror at the situation in which she found herself.

'More than know him?' Connor's swift observation had noted her response, his astute mind processing the implications of it in seconds and coming up with the correct answer. 'Is that the groom?'

With an effort Jenna caught back the groan of despair that almost escaped her. She was trapped; there was no way out and she could only make the best of the appalling hand that Fate had dealt her.

'Yes,' she managed hoarsely, her voice shaking with tension. 'That's Graham.'

CHAPTER SIX

'THAT'S Graham?'

Just for a second, the obvious consternation in Connor's voice broke through the shell of fearful misery that surrounded Jenna.

To her astonishment, she found that she was struggling with a near hysterical desire to laugh, but she was afraid that once she started she wouldn't be able to stop. Even imaginary, the prospect of the awful spectacle of her sitting there, cackling uncontrollably, was enough to sober her up abruptly.

'That's Graham,' she managed to confirm, with only the slightest shake in her voice.

It was enough to draw Connor's eyes to her face in a searing scrutiny that had her tensing again, nerving herself to face a furious outburst. Surprisingly, it didn't come. Instead Connor unclenched his hands from the wheel and turned to look across the road once more.

'He's not at all what I expected.'

The careless words caught Jenna on the raw, combining with her already jittery emotions to produce a combination as volatile as any explosive.

'I'll just bet he isn't!' she erupted furiously, heedless of the way those spectacular eyes had darkened, the tension that held the muscles tight in his strong jaw, drawing the beautifully shaped mouth into a thin, unyielding line. 'So tell me, what did you expect? Some dopey little wimp who couldn't say boo to a goose? Or a short-sighted, balding middle-aged bore who's finally broken free of his mother?'

'Neither—' Connor began, but Jenna was too far launched on her tirade to be stopped now.

'I suppose you thought that because I'd once had you...' deliberately she laced the double-edged 'had' with cruel acid '...no one else would ever seem good enough? That I would retreat into a convent or sell myself into a dull, restrictive suburban marriage where I could eat out my heart with longing...'

'I'd have been a bloody fool ever to think that!' Connor muttered savagely, his eyes fixed on the other man, who was now obviously beginning to wonder why, having parked the car, they were still inside it. 'No one could ever accuse you of any such fanciful ideas.'

But he still hadn't expected Graham to be the tall, dark, imposing man he was.

'He seems to want to talk to you.'

'I know.'

Hunched in her seat, her eyes clouded with misery, Jenna knew she was arousing Connor's suspicions dangerously. But she couldn't face Graham now.

'I'd like to meet him,' Connor astonished her by saying.

'Why?'

The look she turned on him was narrow-eyed and full of suspicion. Just what was he planning now?

'I'd like to see what sort of a person he is,' Connor returned, on a note of innocence that sounded to Jenna's overwrought mind very distinctly out of character. 'Are you coming? He obviously expects you to.'

Try as she might, Jenna couldn't find a reply to give him, at least not one that was fit to use in decent company. Not that she considered Connor decent company, she reflected grimly. But he didn't seem to need any response from her as he pulled the key from the ignition, tossing it carelessly in the air and catching it one-handed as it descended.

'I'll give him your love, then, shall I? After all, he is the man you're supposed to marry in four days' time.'

He was out of the car and turning to cross the road before Jenna's beleaguered brain finally started to work again.

'After all, he is the man you're supposed to marry in four days' time.'

Connor's words repeated over and over inside her head, their ominous implications growing worse and worse with each repetition.

'No, wait! Just a minute!'

In one frantic movement she was out of the car and hurtling across the road after Connor. Her urgency took her halfway towards Graham before she had time to draw breath, and the extra spurt she put on in order to catch up sent her flying over the kerb, tumbling headlong into his arms.

'Jen, love—careful! You nearly landed on that pretty face of yours.'

'Oh, Graham!'

Unthinkingly she flung her arms around Graham's neck, standing on tiptoe to press an enthusiastic kiss against his cheek.

'It's lovely to see you.'

'And you...'

He looked decidedly bemused at her unrestrained greeting, as well he might, Jenna thought ruefully. This was not the sort of response he normally received from her. But she knew that Connor was standing by, a dark, watchful observer of every action, every interplay between them, and that stopped this from being in any way a normal encounter.

'I didn't expect to see you out tonight.'

Graham took a step backwards, settling Jenna securely on her feet before brushing a hand over the sleek darkness of his hair, smoothing it back into place. He still looked slightly wary, as if he was unsure just what she might do next, and her conscience reproved her for putting him in this uncomfortable position. She was taking her own mental discomfort out on him, and it really wasn't fair.

'I thought you'd be at home sorting out the final details of bouquets or hairstyles, or whatever it is that you girls do in the run-up to these events.'

'I—I was…'

Mentally Jenna gave herself a violent shake. Get a grip! She told herself furiously. She was making it painfully obvious that something was wrong, and that was the last thing she wanted.

'But I—I met an old friend. He's staying at the George and we ran into each other there.'

She was gabbling stupidly, her words tumbling over themselves in an effort to avert the storm she felt was brewing dangerously on the horizon. But she couldn't get control of her tongue enough to speak more carefully.

'I thought she looked tired and overwrought—all the wedding preparations,' Connor inserted smoothly, taking matters out of her hands with an efficiency that left her gasping. 'So I invited her out for a meal and a little rest and relaxation.'

'Good idea.' Graham eyed the man who had taken over the conversation with frank curiosity. 'And you are…?'

'The name's Harding. Connor Harding.'

With her heart still thudding unevenly in her chest, Jenna watched as Connor held out his hand and Graham took it in a firm handshake.

'Connor *Harding*?'

'That's right.'

This was how it always had been when someone new met Connor. How she supposed it was every time now. Even people who were not tennis fans had seen his face in the papers, heard of him being trumpeted as the new saviour of British tennis. She had had a tiny taste of such a response herself during those few short weeks when she had been out with him. Wherever they had been there had always been someone who had stared or pointed or wanted an autograph.

Most of them had been women, she recalled, her mouth taking on a bitter twist. They had flocked round Connor, fluttering and twittering like a flight of brightly coloured budgerigars, all vying for his attention.

And Connor had lapped it up, of course. He had enjoyed every moment of it. Those were the sort of females he could handle. The no-commitment, ships that pass in the night, it was fun while it lasted sort of affairs. *They* would never have wanted more, or been foolish enough to let themselves get pregnant so that they threatened to tie him down.

But it hadn't just been the women who had acted like moonstruck idiots when Connor walked into a room. Men too had seemed to fall under the spell of the luminous aura of success that shimmered around him. They admired his physical fitness, his athletic prowess, but most of all they were drawn in by the total self-assurance that he wore with a negligent ease, like the most comfortable, battered casual clothes.

So now she wasn't surprised when Graham, his voice touched with awe, said, 'Connor Harding of Harding's Sports?'

Connor's only response was a curt nod of acknowledgement, but Graham didn't need even that. He was off, launched on his favourite topic—money, and most particularly shares and potential investment.

Well, at least it distracted him from probing any deeper into her supposed friendship with Connor, Jenna thought resignedly. She much preferred this nicely neutral topic to any more contentious subject. But the longer that Connor and Graham stayed together the more fraught the situation became.

She felt as if she was sitting on a keg of gunpowder, watching the flame on a slow-burning fuse creep gradually but inexorably closer. She had no idea when it would all blow up right in her face.

Shifting uneasily from one foot to another, she coughed to draw attention to her forgotten presence.

'Connor…'

His response was immediate. The dark head swung

swiftly in her direction, blue eyes going straight to her face, assessing her mood and summing it up in a split second.

'Getting hungry?' he enquired dryly. 'Then I suppose I'd better feed you. I'm sorry...' He tossed the casual apology in Graham's direction. 'But the table's booked for eight-thirty, and you know what Jenna's like when she hasn't been fed.'

'Of course...'

Graham's response was distracted, his mind obviously still on the facts and figures they had been discussing.

'Well, it was good to meet you...'

Once more that strong-fingered hand was extended, though a certain tension around Connor's mouth left Jenna in no doubt that friendship or even conventional politeness was not what had motivated the gesture. And Connor's next words seemed to confirm as much.

'And I have to say I'm frankly jealous of you.'

'Jealous?' Graham looked completely lost, a puzzled frown creasing his forehead.

'You're a lucky man. You have a very beautiful fiancée.'

'Oh, yes.'

Enlightenment dawned in the same second that Jenna's nerves screamed in panic, the world seeming to swing round her sickeningly.

'Yes, I have. And she means the world to me.' Seeing the smile that lit up Graham's face, no one could doubt the truth of his assertion. 'That's why I can't wait to marry her.'

'Saturday will soon be here,' Jenna inserted hastily, moving forward to enclose him in a swift, warm hug. 'Only four more days to go. I won't see you tomorrow—I have to dash back to London; there are a couple of problems I have to sort out at work. But we'll all be meeting up on Thursday, won't we, for the big family dinner? Now I'm afraid we really must dash. They'll let our table go if we're late.'

She knew that the kiss she blew him as she turned away

was more for Connor's sake than Graham's, but by then she was past caring. She only wanted to get away, escape from the emotional minefield in which she'd been trapped for the past ten minutes or so, and try to bring her frantic thoughts back under control. Coping with Connor on his own was bad enough. Connor and Graham together was more than she could bear.

'You *are* hungry,' Connor laughed as he fell into step beside her. 'Either that or you have a very guilty conscience—'

'I'm starving!' Jenna cut in on him sharply. The state of her conscience was none of his business; not that she was prepared to subject that particular part of herself to any close examination.

She was painfully aware of the way that, behind them, Graham still stood on the corner of the street, watching them walk away.

'I like your fiancé,' Connor stunned her by saying a short time later, when the flurry of activity involved in being shown to their table, presented with the menus and offered pre-dinner drinks was all behind them. 'He seems a very straight sort of guy.'

'He is.'

Jenna used the dark blue leather-bound menu as a defence, carefully holding it up before her face so that he couldn't see her expression as she pretended to be studying it. If the truth were told, she couldn't read a word of anything, the elegantly scripted letters blurring and dancing before her eyes.

'That's what I like so much about him. He's...'

'He's obviously very much more involved in this relationship than you are.'

As Connor reached for his glass and took a deep swallow of his drink Jenna had the distinctly unnerving feeling that in spite of the carefully positioned menu he could still see her face. It was as if that laser-sharp blue stare could burn straight through the flimsy barrier she had erected against him and probe right into her mind, into the heart that was currently performing violent somersaults inside her chest.

'What makes you say that?' The difficulty she was having in breathing naturally made the words come and go unevenly, like the sound on a badly tuned radio.

'"She means the world to me,"' Connor quoted sardonically. '"I can't wait to marry her."'

Behind her flimsy barrier Jenna found that even swallowing hard did nothing to ease the uncomfortable constriction in her throat.

'I think I'll have the chilled soup and the salmon,' she croaked, hoping to distract him.

At least the soup would slip down easily, and she could only pray that by the time her main course arrived she would have relaxed enough to be able to manage it without choking.

'Good choice,' Connor approved. 'In fact it's exactly what I'd decided to have myself. Just the thing for a warm summer evening... Are you planning on changing your mind?' he asked sharply, after a nicely calculated pause.

'No...'

Startled by his unexpected question, Jenna lowered the protective menu until she could see his face, then immediately wished she hadn't. As her disconcerted green gaze collided with his calmly appraising blue one she saw the betraying glint of satirical amusement that revealed only too clearly that he knew exactly what she had been trying to do.

And he had no intention of letting her off the hook that easily. He was clearly ruthlessly determined to make her squirm.

'Then you won't need this any more.'

One long-fingered hand came out and snatched the menu away from her so swiftly that she didn't even have time to form the craven desire to cling onto it, let alone put the thought into action.

For which she should be eternally grateful, she told her-

self a few seconds later, when the instinct to fight had subsided and rational thought reasserted itself. Just the idea of
the sort of spectacle she would have presented, indulging
in an undignified tug-of-war, like a small terrier disputing
possession of a bone, made her cheeks flame in embarrassment.

'Of course not.'

With a struggle she forced a ghost of a smile, so stiff
and blatantly false that she was sure it did nothing to convince him at all, only to have it slide away from her face
with Connor's next comment.

'Now we can have a proper conversation.'

Jenna didn't like to consider what, in his mind, might
constitute a 'proper' conversation. So instead she launched
into another desperate attempt to distract him, divert his
thoughts from the uncomfortable path they seemed determined to follow.

'You surprise me—eating light like that. Anyone would
think you were still in training.'

'Old habits die hard. The few times I've over-indulged
physically I've always regretted it.'

Did he mean in ways other than food? Bitterness ate
away at her heart as she was forced to face the fact that
Connor might consider their past relationship as one of the
occasions on which he had 'over-indulged' and come to
regret later.

'How very controlled of you.'

Unable to meet his eyes, she affected an interest in her
surroundings, studiously concentrating her attention on the
elaborate chandelier in the centre of the room, brilliant
against the gold and white decor.

'You seem to like that in a man.'

Back to Graham again. Obviously her diversion tactics
hadn't worked.

'Do we have to talk about Graham all the time?' she
protested nervously. 'Surely you don't want—'

The arrival of the waiter to take their order meant that

she had to break off uneasily, and once the man had left again she was reluctant to reopen the problematical topic of conversation. Connor, however, obviously felt no such restraint.

'It's very strange,' he murmured, reaching for his glass again. 'Most brides-to-be only want to talk about one thing—their prospective husband—but you seem peculiarly reticent on the subject.'

'I prefer to keep my feelings to myself. I don't go in for the current trend to turn everything into confessional mode—exposing your heart and soul to everyone and anyone.'

'Really?'

One black eyebrow quirked upwards, questioning the truth of her overly vehement declaration. The cynical twist to his mouth set her nerves on edge, driving her to toy restlessly with the array of silver cutlery before her, unable to keep still under his derisive scrutiny.

'You never used to be like that. If I remember rightly, you were only too ready to declare your feelings. You told me you loved me within a week of our first date.'

The pointed barb hit home with a brutal force, stilling Jenna's nervous movements. One hand clenched so tightly over a knife that her knuckles showed white beneath her skin. Hastily she lowered her eyes and stared at the starched white linen of the cloth, hiding her pain behind the veil of her long, thick lashes.

'I was much younger then, and very foolish,' she managed, her voice a blend of misery and defiance. 'I made a very basic mistake—I mistook something shallow and transient for the real thing because I didn't know any better. It was just a schoolgirl's crush.'

'A crush with consequences,' Connor stated pointedly. 'And you were twenty-one—no longer a schoolgirl.'

Luckily for Jenna the return of the waiter with their first course extricated her from the need to find any sort of response to that. When her plate was placed in front of her she could only stare at it blankly, unable even to pick up her spoon.

'It isn't poisoned.' Connor's gentle teasing scraped over nerves already painfully close to the surface, chafing them raw. 'As a matter of fact, it's pretty good.'

The most that Jenna could manage was an indecipherable murmur that he could take as agreement or not, as he wished; she was past caring. Picking up her spoon, she swirled it backwards and forwards through the soup, unable to force herself to even try it.

'Does he know about us?'

Connor's abrupt, sharp-voiced question caught her on the raw, making her start like a frightened cat. The pale green soup splattered onto the white cloth as the spoon dropped from her suddenly nerveless fingers, and she could only stare at the mess in blank horror.

'Jenna?' The single word was a prompt, a reproof and a warning all in one. Connor knew very well that she had heard him, and he wasn't going to let her dodge the question.

Slowly, reluctantly, she raised her clouded green gaze to his.

'He…?' she prevaricated desperately. 'Who?'

Connor's teeth actually snapped together savagely as he fiercely reined in his temper, biting back the enraged retort he had obviously been about to make.

'Don't play games,' he managed after a couple of seconds' unnerving silence, the impact of his words all the more deadly because they were spoken in such a low, ruthlessly controlled voice. 'You know very well who I mean. Your precious Graham—does he know about you and I and what there was between us in the past?'

'No.' It was just a thin thread of sound, barely audible so that he had to strain to hear it. 'No,' she whispered again, before she lost her nerve completely. 'I haven't told him a thing.'

Across the table, Connor's eyes were deep dark pools in

which the flickering flames of the candles in the centre of
their table could be seen reflected. He was suddenly completely still, his face expressionless, the muscles in his powerful shoulders taut underneath the smooth fit of his jacket.
His total silence, the tension that gripped him, seemed to
reach out and envelop Jenna too, holding her frozen, their
eyes locked together.

For a long, soundless second, an electrical charge of
awareness held them, seeming to pulse in the air above the
table. When at last Connor broke the spell by reaching
abruptly for his wine glass Jenna found that her shoulders
sagged weakly, her body aching from being held unnaturally stiffly.

'Don't you think that would be a good idea?' Connor's
voice was strangely rough and husky, as if it came from a
painfully sore throat.

'Oh, there's no need for that.' Jenna aimed for a nonchalance she was far from feeling and missed it by a mile.
'We don't concern ourselves with each other's past. That's
over and done with. The here and now is what matters.'

'How very liberated of you.' It was only too clear that
he didn't mean it as a compliment. 'But aren't you afraid
of how he might react if any—skeletons—do fall out of the
closet?'

'Graham wouldn't hold that against me.'

The thought that Connor could dismiss their baby as a
'skeleton', a sordid, uncomfortable secret that she would
prefer to keep hidden, put a tremor into her voice. And
even Jenna couldn't judge whether it came from anger or
pain.

'Then he's a very rare man indeed. I would never—'

'You would never...?' Jenna echoed, bitterness sharp-
ening her tone. 'Never what? Forgive? Forget? Oh, come
on, Connor! You're suddenly very concerned with the past
for a man who—'

'A man who what?' Connor demanded, when a sudden
thought struck her, stilling her tongue in shock so that she

couldn't complete the sentence. 'Jenna!' he prompted harshly when she could only stare at him, struggling with an idea that was so unexpected it rocked her whole sense of reality.

What if he hadn't known? What if he really was unaware of exactly what had happened? Oh, not the fact that she'd been pregnant. He'd known about that all right, because she'd told him herself. Spilled it all out in a wild, unguarded burst of speech, her heart dying inside her as she'd watched his face pale, seen him take several hasty steps away from her, emotionally if not physically.

But did he know the final tragedy? Did he know what had happened on that bleak, stormy night when she had waited and waited for him to come to her? When she had been so desperate, so needy, that she had ignored the warnings her body was giving her, the dreadful signs that something was terribly wrong.

'*Jenna!*' Connor's voice, raw and abrasive, broke into her thoughts, dragging her back from the bleak horror of the past into the uncertainty of the present. 'What do you—?'

'Did you know?' There was no time to choose her words carefully. No chance to think out what she wanted to say, phrase it delicately so as to take the least risk possible. She could only blurt out exactly what was in her mind, so urgent was her need to be sure. 'Did you know what happened—about the baby?'

If she had lashed out across the table and slapped him hard across one lean cheek the effect could not have been more dramatic. The driven words had barely faded into silence before she saw him withdraw from her. The sensual mouth clamped tight shut, his strongly carved features hardening, closing against her.

In a face that suddenly seemed to be sculpted from the coldest marble, brutal and implacable, his eyes blazed like blue fire, the only living thing in a terrifying death's-head mask.

'Oh, yes, I knew,' he said, each word falling like the lash of whip onto her unprotected soul. 'I knew. Big Brother Grant made it his business to inform me of every last detail. Unless you know of some that he missed, in which case don't hold back...'

'No!'

Only the thought of the other diners in the room kept her still in her seat. The inhibiting effect of their presence and the knowledge that any sort of a scene would be welcome fodder for the greedy appetite of the Greenford scandal grapevine.

Because there would be a scene; she had no doubt about that. If she got up and fled, as she wanted to, Connor would come after her, and his reaction when he caught up with her was not something she could contemplate without a shudder of horror. And so sheer, overwhelming dread kept her frozen where she was when every instinct screamed at her to go, get out of there fast.

'I don't want to talk about it, do you hear?' she declared with a desperate ferocity. 'Not a word!'

She hadn't believed it was possible to detest Connor any more than she already did. That her feelings could grow even stronger, become more extreme. But they did that now, and for a new and shattering reason.

She hated Connor for admitting his guilt. For acknowledging that he had known of the plight in which she had found herself and hadn't done anything about it. She hated him for the callous carelessness with which he had declared that he had learned of 'every last detail', the total lack of penitence or sympathy in the brutal tones of his voice.

But most of all she hated him for the way that by his admission he had snatched away her last remaining fragile hope, sending her plunging into a pit of the darkest despair from which she knew she would never be able to escape.

Only now, when it was finally destroyed, did she realise how her weak, foolish, deluded heart had clung onto the blind dream that perhaps Connor *hadn't* known the full truth. Deep inside she had allowed herself to keep alive the impossible fantasy that, while he had known that she was pregnant and had turned his back on her, maybe, just maybe, he had never learned the full tragic outcome of that pregnancy.

And if that had been so, would he have come to her when he did find out? Would his conscience have been sensitive enough to drive him to want to make amends, even at so late a date? She would never know now, because that last frail hope had died, and with it what was left of her desolated heart, leaving a gaping, bleeding hole where it should have been.

'*You* don't want to talk about it!'

To her consternation, Connor launched onto the attack, blue eyes flashing fire as he leaned forward, his expression so savage that Jenna instinctively shrank back, getting as far away from him as possible while still remaining seated.

'And what if *I* do?'

From somewhere deep inside her, Jenna dredged up the strength to defy him.

'You asked me to have dinner with you, and I'm here. But if you want me to stay then you'd better leave that particular topic where it belongs—in the past. I won't hear another word about it!'

'You find it so easy to dismiss, then? To forget about it?'

'I don't find it *easy* at all!'

She felt as if she was fighting for her life. If he said anything more then she would shatter completely, splintering into a million tiny pieces with little hope of ever being made whole again.

'That's why I want you to shut up. It's either that or I'm out of here…'

'But—'

'I mean it.'

To prove her point she pushed back her chair and prepared to stand up.

'I won't tell you again. That subject is closed, and if you try to open it again I'll leave.'

For the space of six or seven rapid, uneven heartbeats Connor made no response. His stunning eyes, more black now than blue, locked with hers in the flickering candle-light, no hint of softness, of giving in the depths of that obsidian glare. But then at last, unbelievably, Connor sighed and shrugged dismissively.

'All right,' he said flatly, raking both his hands through the ebony darkness of his hair. 'We'll play it your way for now. You can relax, Jenna,' he added pointedly when, still not sure how far to trust him, she remained stiffly perched on the edge of her chair, ready to run if he showed any sign of raking up the appalling subject once again. 'I want you to stay, so I'll obey your rules tonight.'

Jenna didn't like the sound of that 'tonight' one little bit, but at least Connor seemed prepared to make some con-cession, and that was the best she could ask for. Very slowly she let herself relax until she was sitting back in her chair, still watching him with wary green eyes. He met her uncertain stare with a rigidly controlled one of his own, his eyes dead and unresponsive, all emotion blanked off, his thoughts and feelings once more hidden behind the impas-sive mask of a carved marble statue.

'Have some more wine...' In contrast to the unrespon-sive set of his strong features, his voice sounded shockingly normal, casually matter-of-fact. 'You look as if you need it.'

'Oh, come on, Jenna!' he exploded, when she still eyed him mistrustfully. 'You have to make some effort as well. You can't just decree that certain subjects are off limits and then not put anything else in their place! We might as well just pack this in right now and go, if that's the case.'

He was right, Jenna conceded. If they weren't to call it a night right here and now she had to meet him halfway at least. And although leaving straight away, running home and into her bedroom, locking her door so that she could cry her eyes out behind it, was what she truly wanted to do, she was damned if she was going to let Connor see how much he had hurt her.

She had come perilously close to that already, and it was the most dangerous thing she could do. Once he knew that she was vulnerable, that she was on the run from him, what was to stop him from pressing home his advantage with all the ruthless cruelty of a savage predator hunting its prey?

No, she had to stay, no matter how hard it was. Stay and put on a show of carelessness in order to try and convince him that nothing he could do had any effect on her.

And so she forced her hands to stop trembling as she picked up her wine glass and held it out. She even managed a smile.

'You're right. It would be a pity to waste the meal when we've only had a taste of it. And, yes, I will have some more wine, thanks.'

CHAPTER SEVEN

'YOU said you had to go to London tomorrow.'

Connor leaned back in his chair, his cup in his hand, the candlelight gleaming on the darkness of his hair.

'Some sort of problem at work?'

The meal was long over and they were lingering over coffee. In fact, Jenna was stunned to realise, they had been doing so for more than an hour now, talking desultorily, finding a new sort of peace in each other's company.

'Just some documents that need signing and a couple of new projects to finalise. Zoë and Alison have got most things in hand, but there are one or two matters that really need my input.'

'How did you plan to get down there?'

'Train, of course. I don't have a car at the moment. Living in London, I rarely have any use for one, and besides, parking is such a nightmare. So when I come up here I always travel by rail. I can get there and back in a day if I leave at seven.'

A hasty glance at her watch had her grimacing in distaste at the thought of such an early start after what was already becoming a late night.

'Would a lift make things any easier?'

It was a masterpiece of nonchalance. Casually dropped into the conversation, his tone implying that she could take it or leave it; it didn't matter to him.

And so, to her own surprise, Jenna found that her first reaction wasn't to declare that no, there was no way she was going anywhere with him.

Because something had happened in the past couple of hours. Something that had shifted their relationship onto a very different plane, altered her perspectives so that nothing was quite as it had seemed any longer. But it hadn't been like that in the beginning.

At first she had found it very heavy going. She had struggled to respond to the conversational overtures he had made, answer the questions he asked. But she had found that the jittery state of her nerves, the emotional turmoil she was trying to hide, meant that her responses were brusque and abrupt, often downright belligerent.

She had been so sure that in the end Connor would simply give up, convinced that he wouldn't tolerate her bad-tempered snapping and snarling for very long. And it had seemed from his body language—the tight compression of that sensual mouth, the restless tapping of strong, square-tipped fingers on the snowy white tablecloth—that his tolerance level was rapidly being eroded.

But then, just when she'd been positive that he wouldn't take any more, that the evening was completely ruined, with no chance of rescuing it from disaster, he had done something that had stunned her into bewildered silence.

'Hang on a minute,' he said quietly.

And as Jenna watched in blank confusion he took the starched white napkin from his lap, shook the creases from it, and then began to knot it carefully around an unused knife.

'What…?' Jenna's mouth actually fell open in astonishment.

'Sshh!' Connor held a long finger against his lips to silence her, a trace of laughter glinting in the depths of his eyes. 'Wait and see… You'll understand in a minute.'

Privately, Jenna took the liberty of doubting that she'd ever understand anything this man did. But even as she glared at him in suspicion she found her gaze caught and held, mesmerised by the swift, capable movements of those long, powerful hands.

It was impossible not to remember the times when she had known the touch of those hands on her hair, on her skin, on the most intimate places on her body. Her mouth dried, her heart clenching in reaction to the memory of the spellbinding pleasure they could bring, the burning hunger they aroused. Simply recalling it made her skin tingle, as if she had pins and needles all over. Her breasts felt heavy and swollen, the lace top uncomfortably tight against them, and a throbbing pulse had started up low down between her thighs, making her shift uncomfortably in her seat.

What was happening to her? She had always known that Connor had only to touch her and she melted like ice under the sun, but this was different. This was her own thoughts running away with her, the most primitive, carnal responses triggered simply by *looking*, by...

'There!'

The sound of Connor's voice, full of quiet satisfaction, dragged her from the heated delirium of her thoughts. Blinking dazedly, like a small animal caught in the headlights of an oncoming car, she tried to focus on what he held up.

One side of the napkin was now securely fastened to the knife, the rest of it hanging free. As she stared at him blankly Connor waved it aloft, his demeanour totally assured, supremely indifferent to the curious stares of the other diners nearby.

'I don't have a white flag,' he told her, a hint of amusement threading through his voice. 'But perhaps this will do to declare a truce. This constant sniping is getting us nowhere and it's ruining what is actually a fabulous meal,' Connor went on, still brandishing the makeshift banner. 'So why don't we call a truce, just for tonight? Do you agree?'

'I agree,' Jenna managed, the words rather breathless as she struggled with an attack of the giggles that she found impossible to control. 'Anything, if you'll just put down that ridiculous flag! People are staring!'

'Let them!' Connor shrugged off her concern, but Jenna was glad to see that he did lower the knife to the table, where the now crumpled napkin fell in a tangled heap. 'So, do we start again? Pretend the earlier part of tonight never happened?'

If only they could do that with the earlier part of their *lives*, Jenna couldn't help wishing. But that was pure day-dream territory, impossible to achieve. Tonight was different. At least they could salvage something out of the disaster it had been so far.

And so she found herself nodding assent, her smile more genuine this time.

It was easier after that. Gradually she found herself relaxing, opening up more, even enjoying his company. In the space of just a hundred or so minutes, Jenna felt as if she had rediscovered the Connor she had once known—or at least a part of him. The Connor who had entranced and delighted her when she was younger, charming her soul out of her body and enmeshing her heart in love for him.

So now she found she could consider his offer of a lift without the sense of apprehension that might have troubled her earlier.

'It would be a great help, and your BMW is much more comfortable than a noisy rail carriage. But I couldn't ask it of you.'

'You didn't ask; I offered.'

Connor drained the last of his coffee and replaced his cup on its saucer.

'And besides, I wouldn't be making a special journey. It just happens that I have to meet someone in London myself tomorrow, so I'll be driving there anyway. The car has four other seats, the petrol's already been paid for—it seems crazy for you to waste your money on a train ticket when you can come with me for free. Unless your business is so successful that the cost doesn't matter.'

'Quite frankly, I'm in no position to go looking gift horses in the mouth,' Jenna confessed. 'Celebrations may be doing OK, but I've still got to watch every penny. I can't afford to splash out wastefully.'

'Is that a roundabout way of saying you'll come?'

'We-ell, only if I can pay my share of the fuel costs.'

'No way! I invited you; it's my treat. You either come as my guest or...' He made a slashing movement with his right hand. 'The deal's off.'

Jenna couldn't hold back a smile. This was truly the Connor she knew of old. The man who, probably because he had experienced poverty in his youth, had always been absurdly generous with his money once he had it. There were plenty of people in Greenford who had their own stories of a quiet helping hand when they'd most needed it financially, and everyone knew that the prize money from the very first tournament he had won had been used to buy his widowed mother the house of her dreams.

'Come on, Jenny Wren,' Connor cajoled softly, reaching out to lift her hand from the table and curl his fingers round it, warm and strong and so very familiar, reviving memories from long ago. 'Say yes—you'd be crazy not to.'

When he smiled at her like that, the corners of his eyes crinkling into laughter lines at the edges, the deep blue of the irises warmed with golden flecks, Jenna knew she was lost, unable to deny him anything. He had always been able to get round her this way. Always known that she was a sucker for the way that deep, rich voice became a low, husky growl, appeal putting a disturbingly seductive break into its usual confident tones.

'All right,' she said carefully. 'Yes, I will come with you.'

She was rewarded with a wide, dazzling smile, one that winged its way straight to her vulnerable heart and lodged there like an arrow thudding into the gold bull's eye on a target.

Memory was a bittersweet sensation, the taste of honey and acid in her mouth. This was the Connor who had stolen her heart, the man who had first taught her the joys of love, who had opened the door to her deepest sensuality and led her through it. And she had gone willingly, so willingly.

She had delighted in what she had learned at his hands, so much so that she had wanted it to last for ever.

But of course it hadn't lasted. Transient as spring, the glories of that first love affair had withered and died in a frighteningly short space of time. If Connor had taught her joy, he had also brought home to her the anguish of despair, the bitterness of loss. He had driven home the cruel lesson that when only one person loves, when the other is just the loved, giving nothing in return, there is no hope of happiness.

'I knew you'd see reason,' Connor said, and his voice was a tiger's purr, rich with dark satisfaction.

Hearing it, Jenna felt her heart clench in sudden panic at the thought of what she had agreed to. She would be alone with Connor all that time—the length of the journey to London.

But even as fear surfaced rational thought reasserted itself, crushing the sense of dread before it had time to form.

So she would be alone with Connor—but they would be in a car, on the public roads, for heaven's sake! And when the journey was over they would go their separate ways.

She didn't know if Connor planned on coming back to Greenford, but what did that matter? After tomorrow, the wedding would be so much closer. Only a very short time and she would be away, free and clear. Nothing so very terrible could happen in three days, could it?

She could still get out of this. Still change her mind.

For the hundredth time Jenna consulted her watch, only to find that the time had only crept forward by a minute since she had last checked on it. The time she had arranged for Connor to collect her was fast approaching, and she was plagued with terrible last-minute doubts about the whole idea.

Nervously she paced the black and white tiled floor of the hallway, small white teeth fretting at the softness of her lower lip. It was still possible to call a taxi to take her to the station and catch the train. She would be later than she had planned, but that didn't matter.

The sudden sound of a car horn outside told her that any chance of altering her plans had evaporated. Connor was here already, waiting for her.

Outside, the sunlight was already blinding, dazzling her for a moment until her eyes adjusted to it, and she hunted in her pockets for her sunglasses, putting them on as she ran down the steps to the car.

'Hi!' Connor pushed open the passenger door as she approached, greeting her with a wide grin. 'Wonderful day, isn't it?'

'It's *hot*!'

She was grateful for the excuse of the warmth to explain away the sudden rush of colour to her cheeks, the heat that suffused her body as she slid in beside him. The elegant businessman of the previous night had disappeared, and in his place was another Connor, one whose potent, hardcore sexuality was emphasised to devastating effect by the casual clothes he wore.

A soft white tee-shirt and well-worn denim jeans clung to the honed strength of his body in a way that did appalling things to her pulse-rate. The unforgiving close fit of the clothes made it plain that, even though it was more than five years since he had last played tennis professionally, he still possessed the lean power of a trained athlete, without an ounce of superfluous weight.

The blaze of the sunlight through the car's window burnished his dark hair to a highly polished sheen that her fingers itched to touch, to feel its softness slide under their tips. The arms revealed by the short sleeves of his shirt were smoothly tanned, bronze against its whiteness, the fine covering of dark hairs touched lightly by the sun. When he lifted his hands to the wheel, the play of muscles under the golden skin drew her eyes and held them in mesmerised appreciation.

'It's going to get hotter later, according to the forecast.

You'll probably be more comfortable if you dispense with your jacket.'

Jenna had already come to precisely that conclusion. Silently she cursed the need for businesslike tailoring that had influenced her choice of clothes. In contrast to Connor's relaxed comfort, her own coral-coloured linen suit, worn with a toning, paler top, looked stiff and formal, quite inappropriate to the climbing temperatures.

But wriggling out of the long-sleeved jacket in the confined space of her car seat proved a more complicated manoeuvre than she had anticipated, and she twisted and turned ineffectually. The awkwardness of her struggles was aggravated by the knowledge that Connor was watching her, a faint smile curling the corners of his mouth.

His amusement grew into another of those unrestrained grins when she finally ended up completely stuck, her arms trapped behind her, unable to move.

'Well, don't just sit there grinning like an idiot!' Heat and embarrassment made Jenna snappy. 'You might at least help me!'

'You only had to ask,' he returned lightly, blue eyes glinting wickedly and an undercurrent of laughter in his voice.

Leaning forward, he eased the recalcitrant jacket away with a couple of smooth tugs, shaking the folds from it before hanging it over the back of her seat so that it wouldn't crease.

'Thank you,' Jenna managed stiffly, smoothing her ruffled hair with flustered hands. 'I wish I'd never worn the thing. I'll only have to lug it round London all day.'

'You might be glad of it by evening.' Connor was leaning forward to turn the key in the ignition. 'If the predictions of this hot spell breaking prove true, we could be in for some pretty dramatic thunderstorms.'

Every trace of heat fled from Jenna's body, leaving her skin cold and clammy, so that she shivered in distress.

'What's wrong?'

Indulge in a Harlequin Moment.
Anytime. Anywhere.

We'd like to send you **2 FREE** novels and a surprise gift to introduce you to Harlequin Presents®. Accept our special offer today and

Indulge in a Harlequin Moment!

HOW TO QUALIFY:

1. With a coin, carefully scratch off the silver area on the card at right to see what we have for you—**2 FREE BOOKS** and a **FREE GIFT**—**ALL YOURS! ALL FREE!**

2. Send back the card and you'll receive two brand-new Harlequin Presents® novels. These books have a cover price of $3.99 each in the U.S. and $4.50 each in Canada, but they are yours to keep absolutely free!

3. There's no catch. You're under no obligation to buy anything. We charge nothing—ZERO—for your first shipment and you don't have to make any minimum number of purchases—not even one!

4. The fact is, thousands of readers enjoy receiving books by mail from the Harlequin Reader Service®. They enjoy the convenience of home delivery… they like getting the best new novels at discount prices, BEFORE they're available in stores…and they love their *Heart to Heart* subscriber newsletter featuring author news, horoscopes, recipes, book reviews and much more!

5. We hope that after receiving your free books you'll want to remain a subscriber. But the choice is yours—to continue or cancel, any time at all. So why not take us up on our invitation with no risk of any kind. You'll be glad you did!

SPECIAL FREE GIFT!

We can't tell you what it is…but we're sure you'll like it! A FREE gift just for giving the **Harlequin Reader Service**® a try!

Visit us online at
www.eHarlequin.com

The **2 FREE BOOKS** we send you will be selected from **HARLEQUIN PRESENTS**®, the series that lets you meet sophisticated men of the world and captivating women in glamorous, international settings.

Books received may vary.

Scratch off the silver area to see what the Harlequin Reader Service has for you.

HARLEQUIN®
Makes any time special™

YES!

I have scratched off the silver area above. Please send me the **2 FREE** books and gift for which I qualify. I understand I am under no obligation to purchase any books, as explained on the back and on the opposite page.

NAME   (PLEASE PRINT CLEARLY)

ADDRESS

APT.#   CITY

STATE/ PROV.   ZIP/POSTAL CODE

306 HDL C4HJ   **106 HDL C4G9**
(H-P-OS-09/00)

Offer limited to one per household and not valid to current Harlequin Presents® subscribers. All orders subject to approval.

Mentally Jenna cursed the keen awareness that meant Connor had caught her uncontrolled reaction and had turned sharply assessing blue eyes on her suddenly pale face.

'You're not afraid of thunder, are you?'

Not of thunder itself, but of the memories that such weather would stir up. Even now, with the sun blazing down, the air so still that not even a leaf was stirring, she felt sick with apprehension at just the thought of them. And being next to Connor, feeling the heat of his body, the unique, personal, intrinsically masculine scent of him filling her nostrils, only made matters so much worse. Every nerve seemed to be on red alert, screaming with a tension that she couldn't even admit to.

'I don't like storms,' she said carefully. 'When I was a child I used to love them, but when you get older you realise just how much havoc they can cause.'

'When you get older!' Connor echoed mockingly as he put the car into gear. 'Listen to you, Grandma! Personally, I love a good storm. It can flash and bang as much as it likes and I'll be happy.'

He would, Jenna reflected inwardly. Connor had always had a wild, untamed streak in him, one that was more in tune with the elemental forces of nature than the civilised restraints of city life. It was there in the strength of his will, the ruthless determination, the hunger that he had declared was what drove him on. Even as an adolescent he had made it clear that Greenford would never be able to hold him, that he was destined for greater things, that his future would be mapped out on a much wider stage.

'Then we'll just have to agree to differ. After all, we never did like many of the same things.'

'You can say that again.' Connor steered the BMW down the winding drive and turned right into the road at the bottom. 'You always wanted to eat Italian; I preferred Chinese. I loved swimming; you hated to get your hair wet. You could sit for hours reading the longest novel in the world, while I...'

'You always got impatient after ten minutes and wanted to be up and doing,' Jenna finished, the words catching in her throat so that her voice broke in the middle. 'You remember.'

'Remember?'

The swift, sidelong look Connor slanted at her was impossible to interpret. It was only a split second of reaction before he turned his attention back to his driving.

'Of course I remember. You were impossible to forget.'

Jenna snatched in a sharp, uneven breath. 'Impossible to forget', he had said, not 'unforgettable'. There was a major difference in those two meanings, and that difference was like a bruise in her heart.

'And just what does that mean?'

A lift of one square shoulder shrugged off her question.

'Just that you were one of the most contrary, perverse creatures I ever met. Whatever I fancied doing, you were keen on the opposite. The only time we were ever truly in accord was in bed.'

'Now that just isn't true!'

She couldn't bear to let those last two words register, not fully. To think about being in bed with Connor, about making love with him, was more than she could endure right now. It would tear her apart if she let it.

'What about the time that we went walking in the Lake District? We both loved every minute of that. And you enjoyed the ballet... Didn't you?' The twist to his mouth made her suddenly doubt her confident assertion.

'I pretended to for your sake... Oh, don't look so stricken, Jenny Wren! Doesn't everyone do that some time or other? There must have been times when you acted as if you were having a wonderful time when the truth was—'

'No! I never—*never* did that!'

She had never needed to pretend. Every moment she had

spent with him had been so wonderful, perfect in almost every way.

But of course it had never been like that for Connor. *He* hadn't been so deeply in love that he had thought his heart would burst with the joy of it. *He* hadn't found it almost impossible to bear the times they were apart, when each seemingly endless hour stretched out, empty and arid as the desert, until they could be together again.

He had been the love of her young life, the man to whom she had given her heart and her virginity, but to him she'd been only a brief summer dalliance, a pleasant diversion, something to fill the long, frustrating hours until he could get back on a tennis court.

Forced by his injured ankle to hold in check the hunger for success that drove him so hard, Connor had simply directed his energies into another, even more basic appetite. He had gorged himself on her for just as long as it took to satiate the craving, and then he had tossed her aside like a discarded toy.

'I never lied to you—ever!'

'But you lied to Graham. You didn't tell him about us.'

'I told you, he wouldn't be interested!'

'Are you so sure of that?'

Connor fell silent as he concentrated on negotiating the roundabout that led to the motorway, but just as Jenna allowed herself to wonder if he was going to let her off that particular hook he returned to the attack once more.

'What if Graham wants children? Have you talked about that?'

'Of course.' This at least was a question she could answer with confidence. 'He wants a family desperately—preferably two of each. And he doesn't want to wait too long either. After all, he's so much older…'

The words faded into nothing, shrivelling in the blaze of pure fury in his eyes.

'And you don't think that our…'

For once Connor actually seemed lost for words, unexpectedly hesitating over the right phrase to use.

'Our baby!' Jenna flung at him, nausea that had nothing to do with the movement of the car rising in her throat. 'Why not use the word, Connor, instead of hunting around for a polite euphemism? Our *baby*. After all that's what it was. *Our baby!* You see, I can manage it without falling apart.'

'I wouldn't have expected anything else,' Connor muttered savagely, pushing his foot down on the accelerator pedal so that the powerful car leapt forward, flinging Jenna back in her seat with a bruising force.

'There is a speed limit on this road!' she protested, pitching her voice above the roar of the engine. 'I'd prefer it if you'd keep to it!'

'How very cautious you've become all of a sudden, Jenny Wren. How very careful and prudent. But then of course I was forgetting that you're so much older now— much more responsible.'

To her horror he actually took his eyes off the road to look at her, the wild expression in their sapphire depths even more terrifying than the crazy speed at which they were travelling.

'Connor, stop it! You're frightening me!'

'Do you know, I'm frightening myself too?' he tossed at her, with a grim travesty of a smile that had no trace of humour in it at all. 'And it's surprisingly exciting. I haven't felt this good, this *alive* for years.'

But even as he spoke the wild mood seemed to leave him abruptly. To her overwhelming relief he eased up on the accelerator, allowing the car to return to its former relatively sedate pace. The sudden lessening of the tension that had gripped her forced a soft, choking cry from Jenna's lips.

'What on earth possessed you? I was sure you'd kill us both!'

'And you would never take a risk like that,' Connor said,

his tone suddenly strangely flat and lifeless. 'Never put anything as precious as life in jeopardy.'

'No, of course not.' Jenna shook her head dazedly, unable to keep up with his abrupt changes of mood. 'I wouldn't...'

'And Graham? How would Graham react, do you think?'

'I—I don't know. Connor, what is this? Why this—this interrogation? Graham's nothing to you. You can't want to know—'

'Oh, but I do!' Connor's words slashed through hers like a brutal knife. 'I want to know everything. About you and Graham—this man that you're going to marry. I want every last detail. So why don't you start at the beginning and tell me all?'

CHAPTER EIGHT

'BUT why?'

Jenna could only shake her head dazedly.

'Why would you want to know about Graham?'

'Perhaps I'm interested. Perhaps I like a good love story.' The cynicism in his voice turned that statement into a blatant lie.

'N-no...I can't believe that.'

She had no idea what was going on in that incisive, intelligent mind, but she was pretty sure that simple enjoyment of a romance story had nothing to do with it. She wasn't at all comfortable with his concern over Graham. In anyone else she might have put it down as simple curiosity, but not Connor. Connor was never *simply* anything. There was always some deeper motivation at the bottom of his actions.

'All right, then, what if I asked you just to while away the miles? We have a long journey ahead of us; it's going to be very boring if we don't even talk.'

'As I remember, you were never one for small talk.'

Of all the people she had known, he had always been the one who had never seemed to feel the need to fill a silence with unnecessary chatter. He was unusual in that he had been perfectly content to sit in silence with her for long minutes at a time.

In the past she had found that restful. She had even been flattered that he could be so comfortable in her company as not to feel obliged to be something he wasn't. Now, however, just the thought of an extended silence was something she anticipated with a nervous twist in her stomach.

'Come on, Jenna,' Connor coaxed. 'Indulge me on this.'

102

wife, I'd have my ring on her finger before she had time to think. I'd be proud to have her wear it, and I'd hope she'd feel the same.'

'And I'd be proud to wear a ring given to me by the man I loved! But I told you, Graham and I don't need that sort of thing! We don't need gestures or show to—to demonstrate how we feel about each other! We—we...'

'You what, Jenna?' Connor asked dangerously quietly when she floundered, unable to go on. 'You have a wonderful, deep relationship where such things don't matter? You are so secure in each other's love that the usual clichéd gestures are just that—just gestures, meaningless and trite? You—'

'Yes!' Jenna broke in, unable to bear his cynical litany. 'Yes, yes, *yes*! That's exactly right; just how it is!'

'Then why didn't you tell me that? If it's the truth, why didn't you just fling it in my face?'

Because it wouldn't be true, Jenna admitted miserably to herself. Because she and Graham just didn't have that sort of relationship, and if she had tried to claim that they had then Connor would have seen straight through her declaration to the flaw lurking right at its heart.

Because the problem was that Connor expected her to be thinking about Graham all the time. He believed that the other man would be central to her feelings, always there in her thoughts. But the uncomfortable truth was that that was not the case at all.

Much as she hated to admit it, and she found it almost unbearable to acknowledge even to herself, ever since Connor had reappeared in her life she had been unable to think of anything else. Her thoughts, every waking moment, even the few hours' sleep she managed at night, were filled with Connor, Connor, Connor, until there was no room for anything more. Only this morning she had woken, totally unrefreshed, from disturbed and restless dreams filled with fevered, erotically charged images of his dark, powerful presence.

Never before had the luxurious, spacious interior of Connor's car seemed so enclosed, so frighteningly confining. Jenna was more conscious than ever before of the strength in Connor's arms, in his hands on the wheel, the taut muscles in his thighs that tensed and slid as he controlled the powerful vehicle. Hunting desperately for something to distract him from this uncomfortable line of questioning, she seized on the chance offered by a sign for the motorway services with heartfelt relief.

'Would you like to break for coffee?' she managed shakily. 'I could certainly do with a drink.'

With every nerve hypersensitive to even the tiniest thing about him, she was sure that she caught the word, 'Coward!' muttered under his breath. But all the same Connor nodded agreement, and swung the car off onto the side road she had indicated.

Not that she wanted anything to drink, Jenna admitted when they had collected their drinks and were seated at a table in a quiet corner of the restaurant. Her heart was already racing at twice its normal speed, and the effects of caffeine could only make things much worse. And she didn't think she could swallow a single thing. Her throat seemed to have tied itself in knots so that she would choke if she even tried.

Every part of her body was tight with the tension that came with the conviction that Connor would not let the subject of her relationship with Graham drop. A fear that proved to be perfectly justified as soon as he spoke again.

'Perhaps I should talk to Graham myself.'

'Talk?'

Jenna's fingers clenched convulsively on the handle of the cafetière she was holding. Visions of Connor having a heart to heart with the other man filled her mind with fearful dread. Her hand shook so violently that the coffee slopped over the side of her cup, and she had to set the pot down with a distinct crash that earned her a sharp look from those cool blue eyes.

'T-talk about what?' She cursed the way her voice wobbled betrayingly.

Connor waited a nicely calculated moment, stirring his coffee thoughtfully, stretching her overwrought nerves even tighter, before he replied.

'About my finances. If he's as good as you say, perhaps he could give me some advice.'

'You don't need any advice! You have more money than any human being could spend in a lifetime. You don't even need to do another single day's work if you don't want to. You could pack it all in tomorrow and live off the profits you'd made. The interest alone must bring in a fortune a year.'

'I don't need the money,' Connor conceded, with an inclination of his dark head. 'But think how boring life would be if there was nothing to do; no challenges to be met.'

Challenges. A sensation like the slow slither of icy water slid down Jenna's spine so that she shivered inwardly. There before her once more was the cold-eyed, ruthless, driven man she had last seen five years before. This was the Connor who had told her about his hunger for success, the one who had declared that he would let nothing, *nothing* stand in his way.

'You always had to be doing something...'

'I can't stand to be idle. Life is empty unless you're growing, achieving...'

Jenna gave a shaky little laugh.

'What you're doing now is much more the way that the teachers at the school wanted for you. I can remember that most of them—except, of course, Ron Beaumont—thought that you'd wasted your talents taking up tennis.'

'They thought I'd taken the easy way out.' Connor's laughter in return was harsh, splintering the air around them. 'If they only knew. Tennis isn't a game for a kid like me, with no money, no backing. If it hadn't been for Dave...David Curran...my coach, being prepared to take a chance on me, I'd never have got anywhere. He coached me for free and paid my expenses until I started to win enough to actually give him something back. Luckily it wasn't too long before that happened.'

'He had faith in you.'

'And I was determined to justify it. I wanted to prove to him that I was not just a charity case. That I was worth everything he had invested in me. And I don't just mean his financial backing. Dave was like a father to me after my own father died.'

That had been when Connor had been fifteen, Jenna remembered. The cancer that had killed Patrick Harding had been shockingly swift. Barely six months after it had been diagnosed he was dead, leaving his wife and son bereft. She could still recall how her own father had spoken of it. Even he had sounded shaken at the sudden turn of events.

'And now you and Dave are partners. And you're helping other kids like you.'

She'd read of the foundation Connor had set up with his former coach to train and assist talented young players who couldn't afford the expenses of the sport by themselves.

'You have to put something back.' Connor shrugged off the admiration in her voice. 'Are you going to drink that coffee?'

The look he turned on her mug, still sitting untouched on the table, was a pointed reminder of the way that she had expressed such enthusiasm for the drink, only to totally ignore it once she had poured it.

'Of course.'

Hastily she swallowed a mouthful, trying not to grimace with distaste when she discovered how cold it was.

'Did you always plan to go into business when you retired from tennis?'

'I certainly never planned on sitting around doing nothing. A professional tennis player's career isn't exactly a lifetime thing, so naturally I'd made plans. It's just that I had to put them into operation rather earlier than I'd intended.'

And earlier than he'd wanted, Jenna reflected. The damaged ankle that had kept him away from the tennis circuit during their affair had left a persistent weakness, one that had resulted in a further injury just a few months later. An appalling fall had broken his leg, finishing his tennis career well before anyone had expected.

To her consternation she found that tears were swimming in her eyes, misting up the sunglasses she still wore. Blinking hard, she took them off and wiped them clean on her napkin. It was as she looked up again that her gaze was caught by the thin line of the small silvery scar that threaded through one straight black brow.

'Is that a result of that fall, too?'

'This?' Connor lifted his left hand, one long, tanned finger touching the scar briefly. 'No.' His mouth twisted, became a bitter line. 'That's a legacy from a very different occasion altogether.'

His tone grated over her nerves, scraping them raw, making her want to know the reason for it. But the question had barely formed in her mind before it was driven away again by a new and much more disturbing realisation, one that rocked her sense of reality completely.

There was a roaring sound inside her head as she focused on Connor's raised hand. The movement had brought it directly into the path of a shaft of sunlight slanting through the window so that it acted like a natural spotlight, revealing every detail in brilliant clarity. She could see the muscles under the skin, the length of bone, the immaculate square-tipped nails. But what her gaze centred on, staring in blank disbelief, was the faint line, so subtle as to have been unnoticeable before, running around the base of one finger where the skin was not quite so tanned.

Around the base of the *third* finger. The mark was one that could only have been made by a ring; a ring that had been taken off fairly recently. And as the finger was the one where a wedding ring was traditionally worn, that led her to one inescapable conclusion.

'Connor…you're…' she croaked, unable to go any further. Shock had deprived her of all strength, all ability to form any coherent thought. She could only stare, unable, unwilling, to believe the truth of what she saw.

But Connor didn't need her to say anything more. He had caught the direction of her gaze, and his sapphire eyes clouded suddenly, dropping to stare down at his own hand.

'Yeah,' he said harshly. 'I'm married. Correction…' The fingers of his right hand rubbed at the tiny mark, invisible again now that it was out of the direct path of the light. 'I *was* married. The divorce became final six weeks ago.'

It was shocking how much it hurt. Jenna felt as if a cruel claw had just gouged out a piece of her heart, leaving a raw and bleeding wound.

He's married. Married, married, *married*. The words pounded inside her head like a throbbing ache, making her fold her arms tightly around herself in order to counter the dreadful feeling that she might actually fall apart. Even the knowledge that Connor's marriage was now over did nothing to appease the appalling sense of desolation that came with knowing that this man, who had turned his back on her and their unborn child, had once loved some other woman so much that he had made her his wife.

'If I loved a woman and she'd agreed to be my wife, I'd have my ring on her finger before she had time to think.' Connor's words, spoken such a short time before, came back to haunt her now with a force that made the room swing around her sickeningly. He *had* loved someone in a way that he had never cared for Jenna herself.

'Go on, then.' Through the red haze that filled her head, she just caught Connor's words. 'Ask me about her. You want to know… It's only natural.'

And she did want to. That was the appalling thing. The need to know was eating away at her inside. She wanted to know what this woman, his *wife*, had been like. What it was that had made her so special that he had been prepared to commit himself to her, that he had given up that freedom he valued so much?

But she was damned if she was going to let Connor know how she felt. If it killed her she was going to hide the hunger for information from him, making sure that he never glimpsed even a trace of it. To show any interest meant that she cared, at least enough for curiosity, and she *didn't* care, she didn't! She wouldn't even let herself think of it.

And so she schooled her fine-boned features into a mask of pure indifference, blanking off her green eyes as she forced down the disgusting remnants of the now completely cold coffee.

'You couldn't be more wrong,' she tossed at him, in a voice made cold and tight by the control she was imposing on it. 'Your life is your own business. I couldn't be less interested.'

Her chair scraped over the floor as she pushed it back and stood up.

'And now I think we'd better be on our way. I promised my staff I'd be in the office before lunchtime.'

She couldn't look behind, not even to check that he was following as she strode from the room. If she just once met the intent scrutiny of those brilliant eyes she would go to pieces, all her careful discipline destroyed in a moment. She could only move like an automaton, avoiding obstacles and other people by instinct rather than any awareness, her mind refusing to focus on anything but the one devastating fact that had just exploded right in her face.

Back in the car, Connor didn't say a word as they re-joined the motorway, and for a while Jenna was content to let things stay that way. If she never spoke to him again it would be too soon! It was only when she realised that her behaviour was probably having the opposite effect of the one she had intended that she began a hasty rethink.

By reacting as she had she was giving Connor the impression that his revelation about his marriage mattered to her, and that was the last thing she wanted. She wanted him to believe—to *know*—how little it had meant. And so she carefully backtracked, picking up the conversation at the point they had reached just as they'd stopped for coffee.

'If you wanted to discuss investments with Graham,' she said casually, 'I'm sure he'd be only too pleased to help if he could. But don't you have your own advisers for such things?'

'I could hire a whole regiment of them if I wanted.' Infuriatingly, Connor sounded even more off-hand than she had done. 'But I thought that if I talked to your Graham...'

A swift, sidelong glance showed that he had caught the uncomfortable way she had wriggled in her seat at that loaded 'your Graham'.

'I could get to know him better.'

'But why would you want to get to know him? When you leave Greenford at the end of this week you probably won't ever see him again.'

'It's one of the first laws of successful business. Find out all you can about the opposition—the man who has the property you want.'

Jenna knew her jaw had dropped open in shock. She'd asked the question, but she'd never expected such a bluntly candid declaration of intent in response. She could be in no doubt that by 'the property' Connor meant her, that he was still set on winning her away from Graham. The thought of his viewing that prospect in as cold-blooded and calculated a way as a business deal made her skin cold and clammy in spite of the heat.

Well, two could play at that game.

'You've done all the asking so far. It's time I had a turn. About your wife...'

'I thought you didn't want to know anything about her.'

'I've changed my mind.'

Jenna's tongue dripped false sweetness, like honey laced with vinegar. 'Find out all you can about the opposition', Connor had said. Well, she would learn from the master and do just that. She would fight fire with fire if necessary.

'I have to admit that I'm curious as to what sort of woman would be fool enough to marry you. What was her name?'

'Lucy.' He didn't seem so comfortable now that the boot was on the other foot. Jenna couldn't hold back a smile of some satisfaction. The great Connor Harding didn't like having to talk about one of the few failures in his life.

'What did she do for a living?'

'She was a journalist. We met when she came to interview me for the magazine she worked on.'

'How long were you married?'

Definitely not a question he liked.

'Two years.' It came with a snap, like the bite of a trap closing.

'So short a time! What happened?'

'We disagreed over some pretty fundamental things.'

'Like what? Religion? Money? Kids?'

Lean brown hands tightened over the steering wheel, swiftly correcting the faint swerve that was the only indication Connor gave of the fact that her question had hit home.

'Kids. I see. Your wife...' She had to struggle with herself to actually say the word. 'She wanted a family, and you—'

'*She* didn't want one,' Connor cut in sharply. 'That was one of the reasons the marriage was over before it really began.'

'She didn't...' Jenna echoed in disbelief, unable to accept what she'd heard. 'You mean, *you* wanted children? No.' She shook her head, sending her dark hair flying. 'You didn't.'

'Yes, I bloody well did!' Connor's declaration was savage, making her shrink back in her seat. 'I wanted a family; Lucy did not. She didn't want to spoil her figure, or her life. She was totally immoveable on that subject. She'd thought I felt the same way and she could never accept that I didn't.'

Jenna thought she rather understood what the unknown Lucy had felt. Connor had always seemed so single-minded, so totally focused on the success that he aimed for. Marriage had never seemed to play any part in his life, let alone a family. Hadn't she learned that the very, very hard way, when he had rejected her and the baby they had made between them?

But a very short time later he had launched into marriage with another woman. Not only that, but he had wanted a family—wanted it very much, if the vehemence of his response was any indication. The thought was like a cruel knife, stabbing into her heart and twisting hard. Connor hadn't wanted *her* and he hadn't wanted *her* baby, but he had wanted someone else's, there was no escaping the bitterness of that hateful truth.

Connor had turned his back on not just any child but that one particular baby. Her baby. And not just because he'd feared that the effect of the commitment a baby demanded would hold him back in his race up the ladder of success. He hadn't wanted that baby because of who its mother had been. Because it had been *hers*.

He had never loved her, not even the tiniest bit. He had only ever wanted her physically, used her for his own pleasure—as he would do again if she was fool enough to fall for his lies.

'It's all still there between us…needing just a spark…to set it all off again,' Connor had said, and she knew he was right. But the thought of ever experiencing that hunger, that loss of control ever again had her digging her teeth into the softness of her bottom lip in an effort to hold back the cry of pain that almost escaped her. She had barely escaped alive from that maelstrom before. She might not be so lucky a second time.

CHAPTER NINE

'WHAT time shall I pick you up again?'

'Pick me up?' Jenna knew that her doubts showed on her face. 'I thought I'd be going back on the train.'

The last miles of their journey had been completed in the sort of bleak, cold silence that had had Jenna gritting her teeth against the strain of enduring it. She hadn't been able to relax in her seat, and as a result every muscle in her body ached from the tension of being held unnaturally stiffly.

She had found herself praying for the trip to end, counting the remaining miles with an almost superstitious enthusiasm, convincing herself that she could will them to be over more quickly. And when they had finally reached the capital she had asked Connor to set her down at the nearest underground station, saying she would make her own way from there.

'But I thought I'd deliver you to your door.' Connor had finally emerged from the brooding silence that had kept him distant from her for the past three-quarters of an hour.

'There's no need for that,' she'd insisted. That wasn't what she'd had in mind at all. 'It's just a couple of stops on the tube from here. I don't want to take you out of your way.'

To her surprise he had conceded, without the fight she had been nerving herself to face. But now, just as she'd been congratulating herself on escaping comparatively unscathed, he had come out with his question about taking her home again.

'But surely you must have business to attend to, or...?'

'Jenna...' Connor spoke through clenched teeth, obviously reining in the temper that threatened to break away from him. 'I am taking you home again tonight. That isn't up for debate. So you can just stop dancing around the subject and give me a time when we can meet...'

'And what if I don't want to be met? If I don't want a lift home?'

He didn't even deign to respond to her indignant protest, simply looking at the slim gold watch on his strong wrist and doing a quick calculation in his head.

'If we leave at seven we can avoid the worst of the rush hour and still be back in Greenford at a civilised hour. Will that give you long enough to do what you have to?'

'Fine,' Jenna growled ungraciously, knowing she was only banging her head hard against a totally unyielding wall by trying to argue with him. When Connor was set on a course like this there was no swaying him, no matter how hard she tried.

'I thought we'd eat at my place before we left.' Reaching for his wallet, he pulled out a small white business card. 'That address, whenever you're ready. I'll be in all day, so it doesn't matter when you turn up.'

This would be even worse than last night! Just the thought of being with Connor in the intimate surroundings of his home pressed the panic button in Jenna's mind.

'Connor, I don't think—'

'Jenna,' Connor inserted smoothly, cutting off her attempt at protest, 'are you catching the tube or not? I'm sure I could have taken you to your office and back in the time you've spent arguing. In fact...' He leaned forward to turn the key in the ignition.

'I'm going!' Just the thought of him delivering her to her office was enough to have Jenna springing out of the car in a rush. 'But—'

'Can't stop. I'm parked on a yellow line here.' Connor blithely ignored her, lifting a hand in a casual wave as he swung the car away from the kerb. 'See you tonight.'

Oh, damn you, Connor Harding! Jenna actually stamped

her foot hard on the pavement, needing to express her muddled feelings physically. She had been totally steamrollered, with Connor blithely ignoring every attempt she had made to argue with him, sweeping aside anything she'd said that didn't fit with what he had in mind.

But she knew it was far safer to play along for now. If she kept him sweet she would also keep him calm, and that was what she wanted. After all, it was only three days to the wedding now. Even Connor would have to concede defeat and leave if he hadn't persuaded her to change her mind by then. Three days wasn't so long. Surely she could manage to survive until Saturday.

Saturday. Suddenly the day of the wedding seemed a lifetime away. If the past few days were anything to go by, then the next seventy-two hours would be the longest she had ever endured.

Except for the ones she had lived through five years ago, she thought miserably, closing her eyes against the pain that knifed through her. The ones she had spent waiting for Connor, needing to hear from him, praying that he hadn't gone out of her life for good, that he would come back and tell her that everything would be fine now, that he was here to look after her.

She would never forget the way he had reacted when she had told him she was pregnant. With a sob in her throat, Jenna forced her eyes open again, unable to bear the picture that was projected onto her closed lids, the image of Connor as he had been then.

'You're *what*?' he had said, jerking away from her as if he had been burned. His face lost all colour, those amazing eyes burning chips of ice above the high cheekbones where the skin was drawn so tight it was almost transparent. 'Pregnant! But how...?'

'I—I think we both know h-how,' Jenna stammered, with a weak attempt at humour that shrivelled fearfully in the laser-like force of the furious glare he turned on her pallid face. 'After all, we've hardly been out of b-bed...'

'Jenna, don't be bloody stupid!' Connor roared savagely. 'That isn't what I meant and you know it! So now will you kindly explain how you've ended up pregnant when you assured me that—'

'I lied,' Jenna whispered, her voice just a thin thread of sound that he had to strain to hear.

'You did what?'

'I—I lied.'

She was trembling from head to toe, her slender body shuddering in fear and despair. This wasn't how it was supposed to be. She had been so sure, so convinced that when she told him she was expecting his baby, after the initial shock, he would be delighted. She had dreamed of the smile that would light up his face, the joy that would blaze in those brilliant blue eyes. He would gather her up in his arms, hold her close against him...

But holding her close seemed like the last thing on Connor's mind. For all that he was only a few feet away from her, that space seemed to have opened up like a vast, yawning chasm, impossible to bridge. And when she held out her arms to him, pleading for compassion, for understanding, the coldly scathing look he turned on her was as cruel as a blow, knocking them down again as brutally as if he had struck her.

'I—I know I told you that you didn't need to take precautions...' With a monstrous effort Jenna swallowed down the tears that clogged her throat, threatening to choke her. 'That—that I was on the pill. But I was—sort of jumping the gun a bit.'

'*Jumping the gun?*' Connor's caustic repetition of her foolish words made her wince in distress.

'The truth is that I never expected things to go that far that fast.'

Emerald eyes pleaded with him to believe her. To understand that she had never actually believed that after that one time he had taken her out to say thank you, three years before, Connor Harding, the tennis world's brightest star,

and already a millionaire, would ever look again at the
homely girl he had so laughingly nicknamed Jenny Wren.

She had been stunned when he had asked her out again,
even more amazed to find that when that date was over
he'd wanted to see her again. Every time she saw him after
that she had expected him to say it was over, that he was
bored, and so she had been totally unprepared for the night
when he had made it plain that he wanted to take things a
whole lot further. By then she had been in so deep that the
idea of saying no had never even crossed her mind.

'I didn't think you would want me—physically, I
mean...' Her voice deserted her as she saw the way his
head went back sharply.

'Don't be ridiculous, Jenna! You've grown into a beautiful woman; you must know that.'

'You made me feel beautiful.'

Foolishly she let herself believe that the harsh-voiced
compliment meant that he was softening, that his animosity
towards her was lessening.

'And when you kissed me I went up in flames. I couldn't
breathe, couldn't think. I only knew I wanted you so much
that I thought my heart would break if you didn't...'

'So instead you put both our futures at risk because of
your silly lies. And you told me you were a virgin,' Connor
continued callously. 'Or was that a lie too?'

The pain was unbearable, all the more so because she
knew that it was her own foolishness that had left her open
to it. Desperately she opened her mouth to refute the terrible accusation, only to find that her throat had closed up
in anguish and no words would come.

'You've already admitted that you lied to me once,'
Connor went on, the anger evaporating from his voice and
leaving in its place a glacial control that was more terrifying than his earlier rage. 'Why should I believe your word
on anything else?'

'Because it's the truth—you know it is!' Despair slashed
at her savagely as the cynical lift of one dark brow ques-

tioned the sincerity of her declaration. 'Connor, you have
to believe me. I didn't mean to lie. I fully intended to sort
out contraception—I did, just as soon as I could, but by
then it was too late.'

'Too late.' Connor pounced on the words like a hunting
cat on its prey. 'So now you're saying you fell pregnant
the very first time we—slept together.'

And if Jenna had needed any clear evidence of the difference between the way Connor thought of their relationship and her own feelings, it was there in that uncharacteristic hesitation, the telling use of that single phrase.

To her, lost in the throes of her first real love, having
given her heart to Connor in the first moment that she had
met up with him again in the local record store, the physical
side of their relationship could only ever be described as
'making love'. But in Connor's mind they had simply 'slept
together', a purely physical act without the emotional implications that meant so much.

'Why not just call it having sex?' she flung at him, her
own anger sparking now.

'Oh, so you didn't like that?' Connor's keen ears had
caught the faint gasp of protest she had been unable to hold
back. 'But why be so prim, darling? You needn't be afraid
to call a spade a spade. This is the nineties, Jenny Wren.
Women are allowed to feel things like desire and passion
without having to pretend to other emotions to excuse them.
You don't have to hide behind the façade of being in love
in order to—'

'I'm not hiding!' Jenna protested vehemently. 'And it's
not a façade! I *do* love you!'

'Well, don't expect me to reciprocate in kind,' Connor
tossed back heartlessly. 'Because if you do you'll be bitterly disappointed.'

The effect of those coldly indifferent words was as
shocking as a slap in the face, bringing her up sharp against
her own foolish naivety. Belatedly Jenna realised that she
had been playing this all wrong. She had been behaving

like an unworldly, small-town girl, with her heart, all her feelings on display. The sort of sophisticated, cosmopolitan women that Connor was used to would have handled things much more calmly, showing a great deal more composure.

Drawing on her fast-dwindling reserves of emotional strength, she stiffened her spine and lifted her head to meet his freezing blue gaze head-on.

'Of course you don't have to love me, Connor.' She was proud of her voice. It sounded a perfect match for Connor's own; not a trace of a tremor to reveal her inner torment. 'But we do have to decide what we're going to do.'

'Do?'

Jenna allowed a faint smile to escape her at Connor's blank echoing of her last word. This was better. He actually looked slightly dazed, as if stunned by this new and very different Jenna.

'Well, of course. It seems to me that we have only two possible alternatives. Marriage, or...'

She couldn't even voice the second option because she could never, ever consider it. It was impossible to think of aborting her child.

'And naturally I would prefer marriage.'

'Naturally.'

Jenna was concentrating too hard on keeping control over her emotions to take any heed of the cynical interjection.

'Of course my father won't be too pleased...' He'd be furious. Her blood ran cold just to think of the force of his probable reaction. 'Or my mother. But I'm sure I can talk them round. If we marry soon, no one need ever know. I'm only six weeks now; I won't start to show for ages yet. We can say that you have to be away on tour very soon, and that will explain the rather hasty preparations. We can be married in St—'

'Very neat.'

Her voluble flow of ideas was harshly interrupted, bringing her up sharply.

'What?'

'You've got it all planned out very thoroughly.' Connor's tone took his statement to a point light-years away from a compliment. 'Almost all the loose ends tied up. But you've forgotten one important thing.'

'And what's that?'

'A groom.'

'A *groom*!' Jenna actually laughed; the idea was so absurd. 'Oh, don't be ridiculous, Connor! Obviously you'll be the groom. Who else...?'

'I don't recall ever proposing marriage.' Each word was curt and clipped, falling on her sensitised skin as if formed from drops of ice. 'So you see, Jenna, darling, if you want this fantasy wedding you've dreamed up to go ahead, you're going to have to find someone else to stand in as the happy groom.'

'But...but...' Every thought of control, of behaving like the worldly-wise female he expected, fled from Jenna's mind, swept away by a tidal wave of shock and disbelief. 'But you can't! I won't let you! You have to—'

'One thing you should learn about me, Jenny Wren—' Connor's words slashed through her incoherent tirade '—is that I never *have to* do anything. I do only what I choose— what suits me.'

'And it doesn't *suit you* to marry me?'

'Can I get back to you on that?' His casual drawl was the final insult, revealing total indifference to her plight and the way she was feeling. 'Say by the end of the week?'

'No!' Beyond caring what he thought of her, Jenna stamped her foot in petulant rage. 'You tell me now or it's all over between us. Do you hear...?'

'Fine.' A shrug of his broad shoulders dismissed her fury as irrelevant.

He had actually turned and was walking away before she quite realised what he intended. For a couple of blank, bewildered seconds, she could only stare in stunned disbelief.

'Connor! Don't do this! You can't! You have to—'

'I told you, darling...' The words were tossed over his shoulder to her. 'I don't have to do anything. But if I do decide to, then I'll let you know.'

'Excuse me!' The pointed words penetrated the trance that had held Jenna frozen, dragging her back to the present and away from the pain of memories she hadn't wanted to recall.

'Oh, I'm sorry!'

Realising that she had been standing, lost to the world, in the entrance to the tube station, partially blocking the way of other would-be travellers, she coloured in embarrassment. She had to pull herself together. Heaven alone knew how long she had been here.

Hastily she moved out of the way, shaking her head to rid her thoughts of the last unwanted echoes of the past that clung there like sticky cobwebs. She had to get back in control of her life, and getting to the office was the first step. She was late enough already. Alison and Zoë would think she wasn't coming.

And after work she knew just the thing that would relax her and give her new confidence to face Connor once again. Squaring her shoulders and lifting her chin determinedly, she headed for the ticket machines.

'You look amazing! What have you done to yourself?'

Connor's reaction when he opened the door to her that evening was everything she could have wanted. The sapphire eyes gleamed in stunned admiration, their pupils widening until there was only the faintest rim of bright colour at the edge of the black.

'Do you like it?'

Intoxicated by the heady effect of his approval, Jenna pirouetted in order to give him a clear view of the full effect, her hands going up to the smooth bell of her hair that now hung sleek and elegant, a good three inches shorter than before.

'I didn't actually plan on having so much cut off, but when Adam suggested it I thought—why not? It is so much more stylish this way.'

Which was something she had been glad of when she had finally reached the imposing building where Connor had his London apartment.

She should have known, of course. Should have realised that the Connor Harding of Harding's Sports he had become wouldn't live in some shabby bedsit or a run-down terrace house. But all the same she had been unprepared for the impressive entrance hall with its marble floors, and the security guard who had checked her name against a list at his desk before allowing her into the private elevator that had carried her all the way up to the top floor.

She had never anticipated this enormous open-plan apartment, furnished in blond wood and cool, natural colours, its living area alone big enough to swallow up the whole of her own small one-bedroomed flat. From the huge plate glass windows she could see the whole of London spread out below her, the people and cars as small as ants, the sound of the traffic silenced by the distance.

'And much cooler, of course, which is a major consideration today. Though it's much more comfortable in here.'

'The apartment is fully air-conditioned. But all the same, I take it a cold drink would be welcome?'

'It would be wonderful!' Jenna said gratefully. 'I'm parched!'

'Sparkling mineral water—a couple of slices of lemon and lots of ice?'

'That sounds perfect.' Jenna followed him into the streamlined, ultra-modern kitchen and perched on a stool as he opened the fridge, pulled out a bottle and opened it with a hiss of escaping gas. 'I reckon it must be hot enough to fry an egg on the pavement out there.'

The heat had been building all day long, growing more

and more oppressive with each hour that passed, and even the coming of evening hadn't reduced the temperature in the slightest. But at least the storms that Connor had predicted hadn't arrived, for which she was heartily grateful.

'Well, this should help.'

'Thanks!' Gratefully she accepted the tall glass, beaded with moisture, and swallowed the ice-cooled water appreciatively. 'That's better. I feel much more human now—not the sweaty mess I was when I arrived.'

After a day in the soaring temperatures, she felt as limp and wrung out as an old rag. Connor, in contrast, looked perfectly cool and composed.

'Don't fish for compliments,' Connor reproved with a smile. 'You look stunning, and you know it. But I must say that you're a most unusual woman.'

'Why's that? Because I've had my hair done? That's nothing…'

'Because you've had your hair cut so close to your wedding day. I would have thought— Steady!'

Moving forward hastily, he took the glass from her hand as Jenna choked on an imprudently deep swallow of the sparkling water.

'The water went down the wrong way,' she managed, when she at last she could speak.

She couldn't believe what she had done, couldn't imagine how it had happened. She had actually *forgotten* about the wedding! How could she have done that?

She had been so determined to boost her self-esteem, had wanted so much to do something to impress Connor that it had driven every other thought from her mind. Now reality came rushing back at her with a force that made her head reel.

Desperately she pictured the head-dress she and Susie had chosen together, trying to imagine how it would look with her new hairstyle. Would it still work? Susie would kill her if it didn't! She had very set ideas about how her sister was to look on the big day. And the hairdresser who had been booked for Saturday morning wouldn't be best pleased either. The elegant braid they had decided on would probably not be manageable now that her hair was so much shorter.

'I'm fine now,' she said edgily, anxious to have Connor look somewhere else. 'Really—completely recovered.'

'Good.' His smile did dreadful things to her already unsettled pulse-rate, making her heart skip a couple of beats and bringing a flare of colour high up on her cheeks. 'So what would you like to do now? Are you ready to eat or would you like to see round the flat first?'

The meal would be the most sensible course, Jenna told herself. It would be much the safest move to eat as quickly as possible and then get out of there. But if she was honest she was frankly intrigued to see the way that Connor lived now. She wanted to know more about him, and what better way to do that than to explore his home? Curiosity fought a nasty little battle with common sense, in which the more prudent option never even stood a chance.

'I'd love to see round your home,' she said brightly. 'Are the rest of the rooms as spectacular as these?'

'Come and see.' Connor ushered her out of the kitchen. 'Then you can make up your own mind.'

Half an hour later, Jenna was speechless with pleasure, unable to express her enchantment with everything she had seen. If the living area had been impressive, then the rest of the rooms that opened out from that centre were perfection itself. There was even a terraced roof garden, a green oasis in the middle of the city where, with the bustle of the streets muffled far below them, it was possible to imagine that you were actually in the calm of the country.

'It's wonderful!' she exclaimed, slightly breathless with delight. 'Absolutely gorgeous! You must love living here.'

'Well, actually I prefer the estate I have in Suffolk— that's where my mother lives now. But if I have to be in town then this place suits me.'

'An estate!' Jenna teased archly, green eyes gleaming. 'How things have changed. Are you trying to impress me?'

'Do I need to?' Connor shot back, the brusqueness of his reply sobering her slightly.

'Of course not...'

He had never had to try to impress anyone. Connor had always been extraordinary enough just by existing. Aside from his looks, his brilliant talent for tennis and the keen, incisive mind that had ensured that when one career ended he could create a second, even more successful one as a businessman had always ensured that he would stand out in any crowd.

'But I am trying to explain,' Connor astounded her by continuing. 'You had money and comfort all your life. You never knew what it felt like to feel the hunger, to be driven by ambition to change your status in life. All those years ago, I *wanted* this, and I was prepared to do whatever it took to get it.'

Whatever it took. The words echoed bleakly inside Jenna's head. Even to walk away from your unborn child.

'There's one door here that we haven't opened.' Desperately she tried to distract him, to bring the conversation back onto a level she could cope with. 'What's in here...?'

Her voice died as she focused on what could only be Connor's own bedroom, The navy and white décor was uncompromisingly masculine, and a denim shirt lay carelessly discarded on the bed, a pair of shoes on the floor.

Suddenly she was assailed by a terrible feeling of panic. There was no escaping the intimacy of her surroundings. Connor's character was stamped onto every detail, from the book on the bedside cabinet to the handful of change dumped on the dressing table, the hairbrush lying beside a bottle of his favourite aftershave. If she inhaled she could breathe in its scent, so hauntingly familiar, so evocative of memories from the past.

Five years ago she had been so well acquainted with

every detail of Connor's room at his mother's house. She had had the freedom to wander in there whenever she'd wanted, touch anything she'd liked, and she had always felt safe, so much at home. But that had been when she had believed he cared for her. Now she felt totally wrong, alien, an intruder.

Whirling round in distress, she slammed straight into the hard wall of Connor's chest, all her breath escaping from her in a shocked gasp.

'I'm sorry...I...' The words dried on her tongue as she saw the expression on his face, the darkness of his eyes.

'Do you know how long I've dreamed of having you back in my bedroom, Jenny Wren?' His voice was softly husky, coiling around her like warm smoke, weaving a sensual spell in her mind. 'How many nights before I go to sleep that I shut my eyes and see you here, close enough to reach, but know that you're only a dream? Do you know what it does to me to realise I've just imagined you, that if I stretch out a hand and try to touch you—'

'Connor, no!'

Jenna couldn't bear to hear any more, couldn't risk letting that hypnotic voice sink into her consciousness. If she did, she knew it would drive away all reason, all sense of self-preservation, destroy all control. Already her breathing was quickening in time with the thud of her heartbeat, liquid heat flooding her veins, setting her whole body tingling in sensual response.

He was so close that she could hear his breathing, feel the warmth of his strong body. That unforgettable combination of the so-familiar aftershave and the warm, clean scent of his body filled her nostrils, making her head spin with the hunger that spiralled deep inside her.

'Don't!'

Desperately she looked round the room, hunting for a further distraction from this potential danger. She found it on the far windowsill, a small silver-coloured cup, worn and shabby, its cheap metal and plastic base oddly out of place amongst the otherwise luxurious surroundings.

'The school tournament trophy!' Crossing to the window, she picked it up, turning it round in her hands, not quite believing what she saw. 'You kept it, after all this time.'

'Of course.'

She hadn't got away from him. He had followed her, and now stood even closer beside her. She felt his presence like a glowing aura that reached out to surround her, enclosing her in a pulsing sense of awareness, bringing every nerve, every cell to greedy, clamouring life.

'I keep it to remind me of how it all began, of what I was, where I came from. Tell me...'

Reaching out, he took the cup gently from her unresisting grasp, Jenna's fingers too having fallen under the spell he cast, so that they were incapable of movement, of response, unless he commanded it.

'Did I ever really thank you for the way you helped me that day, for borrowing Grant's racquet for me?'

Jenna's smile flashed on and off like a neon sign, her laughter shaky and strained.

'You mean, apart from the drink you bought me years later? I think you flung a casual "Thanks, kid" in my direction. You ruffled my hair too, before you dashed off to the first match.'

The smile on Connor's beautiful mouth was wryly self-deprecating.

'I was a real charmer in those days, wasn't I? No social graces at all. But I want to make up for it now...?'

The silver cup was tossed to one side, landing on the cushioned softness of the duvet on the bed, and Connor's grip, warm and strong, closed around the hand that had held it.

'I want to thank you properly for what you did that day...'

Her fingers were lifted until they were level with his

mouth, and with an aching jolt of her heart she felt the heat of his lips against her skin. But she couldn't look down because Connor held her wide-eyed gaze with his own, his blue stare blazing with a golden fire that was hotter than the sun still streaming through the window behind her. That heat pulsed through her body, centring at the most intimate point between her thighs.

'You took a real risk.'

A soft kiss landed on her thumb, making her stomach clench in instant response.

'I—I didn't, really. Grant…'

The exquisite sensation of the moist warmth of his mouth on the next finger made it impossible to go on.

'Grant was never the push-over you believed him to be…'

'Connor…' It was a choking cry. 'Don't talk about Grant now, about the past.'

'You're right.' Husky and deep-voiced, it was spoken with the strength of conviction, punctuated by further kisses dropped onto the three remaining fingers. 'It should stay in the past. What matters is right here and now and what there is between us.'

'And that is…?'

'Oh, Jenna!' Connor's laugh was low and sensual. 'You know. You've always known. It's just you were running scared before. Too scared to admit to what you were feeling—to what you need.'

Her imprisoned hand was turned until it was palm uppermost, his fingers smoothing over the soft skin. Then, as Connor bent his dark head and pressed a lingering kiss in the very centre of her sensitised flesh, Jenna could not hold back a moan of response that was a sound of pure hunger.

His face seemed so much closer now; that sensual mouth only inches away from her own. And, looking deep into those burning sapphire eyes, Jenna saw the change in them. She saw the way that awareness became arousal, need transmuted into an inferno of hunger raging out of control.

She saw these things and recognised them, knowing that they were there in her own eyes too.

Slowly she reached out and touched the lean plane of his cheek with hesitant fingertips, her eyelids half closing in ecstatic response to the feel of the warmth of his skin against hers.

'I'm not running scared now, Connor,' she whispered. 'And I know exactly what I want.'

CHAPTER TEN

'SO WHAT do you want, my Jenna?' Connor's question was a deep, sexual growl. 'Tell me what you want—whatever you want—and I promise you, you can have it. If it's in my power to give it you…'

'In your power!'

Jenna's unsettled laughter broke through any attempt at restraint. Not that she was capable of any sort of control. She was lost, adrift on a heated golden sea of desire, totally at the mercy of the hunger that was throbbing inside her, beating at her temples so that it was impossible to think of anything else.

'Oh, Connor, of course it's within your power! In all this world, you are the only one who can give me what I need.'

'Then tell me what you want. Put that need into words… No?' he questioned softly, when she could only shake her head, her control over her voice lost completely. 'Then let me make it easy for you. Is this what you want?'

His lips brushed her forehead, sweeping aside the smooth fall of her silky dark hair.

'Do you want my kiss here…or here…?'

That gentle caress moved lower, sliding over the delicate skin of her cheek, lingering briefly on her lowered eyelids, drawing a whimper of response from her, making her stir in restless reaction.

'Yes?' Connor whispered. 'Is that what you want?'

'Oh, yes…' It was just a sigh.

'And do you want my touch on your face…?'

Long, powerful fingers splayed out across her jaw, their innate strength carefully tempered into an extraordinary gentleness that made tears of delight prick at her eyes.

'On your neck...'

The slightly roughened fingertips moved softly down her throat, making her arch her head backwards in instinctive response to the delicate sensation.

'Or your breasts...' And his hands slid lower, to close over the soft swell of her breasts, his thumbs finding and teasing at the straining points of her nipples.

Jenna's moan was a sound of rapture, of surrender and demand all at once. She wanted him to know how he was making her feel, needed to abandon herself to his strength and masculine potency. But she also wanted more. More than just the limited caress of his hands through the barrier of her clothes. More than the tantalising temptation of kisses that tormented her lips with promises then danced away again to subject her temple, her eyelids, even the delicate lobes of her ears to butterfly-light enticement.

She wanted the true force of this man's desire, hard and strong and passionate. The compulsion was so deep, so raw, that it was like a wild electric current flaming along the pathway of every nerve in her body, making her writhe in restless excitement against the taut, powerful contours of his lean frame.

'Connor...' His name escaped on a cry of need, forced from her lips by a hunger she could no longer control, and, hearing it, Connor laughed roughly deep in his throat.

'Say it, Jenna,' he urged. 'Say what you want. Tell me how to please you.'

His body seemed to be on fire, the sleek, bronzed skin of his arms and chest burning through the clinging white cotton of his tee-shirt. High on the carved cheekbones, a streak of heightened colour scorched his skin under the febrile brilliance of his eyes. His breathing rasped, raw and uneven, with the effort it took him to drag air into his lungs. And, held as close to him as she was, she couldn't escape the heated, forceful evidence of the passion that flamed in his blood.

'I want... I want...'

'*Say it!*' His voice rasped in her ear, throaty and shaking, on the edge of control, his breath hot on her cheek. 'Jenna, for God's sake...'

'I want you.'

There, it was out and there was no going back. Jenna sagged against him in relief at being able to admit to the truth at last, to acknowledge the emotions that had been building up inside her like the molten lava inside some powerful volcano, threatening to erupt violently at any moment.

'I want you to—'

'Lady, your wish is my command!'

With his arms around her waist he lifted her off her feet, and in a movement that was like some primitive form of love-dance half-carried, half-swung her towards the bed, his mouth plundering hers all the while.

'If you only knew how I've wanted this,' he muttered against her lips. 'How many times I've thought of how good we were together and dreamed of knowing your glorious sensuality once again. Oh, Jenna...'

Slowly he put her back on her feet, letting her slide down the shuddering length of his body as he lowered her to the floor.

'You must know what you do to me—feel how you affect me.'

'I—I know,' Jenna managed on a shaken laugh. 'How could I not when— Oh!'

Her uneven words broke off on a cry of shock and confusion as an unwary step backwards produced a disturbing crunching, the ugly splintering of broken glass.

'What was that? What have I done?'

'Leave it!' Connor shook her slightly, wanting to bring her focus back to him. 'Whatever it is, it doesn't matter.'

'But, Connor, I've broken something! I can't...'

Twisting away from his grasp, she dropped down onto one knee on the carpet, slipping her hand under the bed to retrieve the damaged object.

'I think it's a picture frame or something. I'm afraid I've ruined the glass, but the photo… Oh, my God!'

The cry was wrenched from her as the object finally emerged into the light and she saw what it was. All colour seeped from her face as she stared down in horrified disbelief, unable to accept what she was seeing.

Behind her, Connor froze, then launched into a violent string of curses, venting his feelings in a stream of dark eloquence whose baleful force was almost physical in its impact.

'Connor?' Still Jenna couldn't look away, her gaze held transfixed, her mind rejecting the evidence of her own eyes.

'Jenna, give that to me!'

Connor's hands closed over the framed photograph and wrenched it from her slackened grasp, flinging it aside with a force that had it crashing hard into the opposite wall and splintering even more. Tiny shards of glass dusted the rich blue carpet and lay there sparkling like miniature diamonds.

'Connor… What…?'

Her movements slow and unnatural, like a film slowed down and played at the wrong speed, Jenna turned towards him, staring up from her position on the floor, dazed green eyes pleading for an explanation.

'Who…?'

But even as she formed the question she knew the answer. And if she'd ever doubted the accuracy of her unwilling conjecture, then a single glance at his face told its own story.

Where his skin had been flushed before, now it was the colour of parchment, and harsh lines of strain and tension were etched around his nose and mouth, making him look much older than his years. His eyes were hooded, all emotion blanked off, as if tempered steel shutters had just come down behind them, concealing his thoughts from her. And the wide, sensual curve of his mouth was clamped into a brutal, unyielding line. There was no chance of any weakness in the form of emotion escaping from its rigid control.

'Jenna, I told you to leave it! It's not important! It doesn't matter...'

He moved to take her hand, meaning to pull her up from her kneeling position, but she snatched it away, clutching it to her as if his touch had burned her skin.

'Not important!' It was a cry of pain, wild and high-pitched, like the sound of a small animal caught in the cruel jaws of a trap. 'It doesn't matter! But if that was who I think it was then it *does* matter! It matters one hell of a lot!'

'Jenna...' The use of her name was so very different now, the deep voice sounding a warning, no longer a protest. 'Don't ask.'

But she had to ask. Even though she already knew what the answer would be, she had to be sure. Had to hear his voice confirm her suspicions, see his face as he told her.

'Connor...'

Holding onto the bed for support, she got slowly and unsteadily to her feet, weakness making her sway slightly, not at all sure that her cotton wool legs would actually support her.

'Tell me the truth. The woman in the photograph. Is that—'

'Yes,' Connor cut in heavily, not needing her to complete the question. His eyes were very dark and shadowed, looking bruised against the pallor of his skin. 'Yes, that's Lucy. My wife—ex-wife for the past six weeks.'

It was only what she'd expected, so why did it hurt so badly? She had thought that she had been prepared for it, that she had nerved herself for the pain his answer would bring.

But nothing could have prepared her for this. Nothing could have armoured her against the agonising, burning, tearing sensation that felt as if a white-hot knife was slashing into her soul again and again, inflicting the most hideous wounds it was possible to endure and still remain alive.

But of course the anguish was only mental, not physical. A heart didn't actually break in reality, however much it might feel as if it had. She had to suffer it, and still remain aware of what had happened.

'She...'

She had to swallow hard to force down the knot of agony that was closing off her throat, forcing her to breathe in great gasping breaths, dragging the air into her lungs with a terrible effort.

'She looks... No, *I* look like her.'

She changed the emphasis deliberately, and knew that her reasons for doing so had hit home when she saw his dark head go back sharply, as if he had been struck in the face, something dangerous flaring deep in his eyes.

'*Just* like her!' To her relief her voice had gained some strength, no longer coming and going like a wave lapping against a shore. 'In fact, I could be her double.'

'No...' Connor interjected hoarsely, taking a hurried step towards her, his hands coming out to take hold of her arms.

But Jenna slapped those grasping fingers away, astounding herself as much as him by the way she found the strength to repel him in this way.

'Don't touch me!'

The wildness in her eyes stilled him where her tone was not quite strong enough. Her head was held high, chin lifted defiantly, a desperate bravado holding her slender body stiffly erect.

'Don't you dare come near me—do you hear? Not now, not ever!'

'Jenna,' Connor protested, gentling his voice in an effort to appease her. 'You've got it all wrong.'

'Wrong!' Jenna echoed, lacing the word with bitter mockery. 'Is that so? So tell me, Connor, how wrong have I got it? It all seems so very clear to me. This—this Lucy...was your *wife*. The woman you loved enough to marry...'

Oh, how it hurt to say that.

'But the woman who left you because you—disagreed over "some pretty fundamental things".'

'Jenna…' Connor tried again, but she was too far gone to be stopped.

'The woman who hasn't been in your bed for months. You must be hellishly frustrated, Connor. Desperate. And is that where I came in? If you couldn't have the genuine article, you'd settle for a substitute? Second-best.'

'Don't be stupid!'

'Oh, don't try to cover your tracks now, Connor, it's way too late! I've seen right through your nasty little scheme— thank God I caught on before I really had something to regret. Because there's something you should know—I'm no replacement for anyone, no stand-in, and definitely never second-best! I'm me and I'm totally unique, and far too good to waste on a rat like you.'

'You…' Connor began, but this time his move forward was positively the last straw.

Unable to take any more, Jenna whirled, and fled, snatching up her bag and dashing out of the apartment. She was in the lift, stabbing a frantic finger on the 'down' button even before Connor made it to the hallway. The last thing she saw was the furious expression on his face as the doors slid shut and she finally made her escape.

The storm that had been threatening all day finally broke just as Jenna's train left the station. For a while now the skies had been growing darker and darker, the humid heat becoming unbearably oppressive. And Jenna had felt the pressure building up inside her head, creating a blinding headache that was like a steel band fastened round her skull and twisted tighter and tighter until it dug in at her temples.

But in the moment that the first crack of thunder could be heard, the flash of lightning streaking across the sky, she had been flung into a frenzy of panic in which her heart pounded at three times its normal rate. Her breathing became raw and jagged, and her head swam with the effort it took to remain in her seat, maintaining an outward appearance of calm in contrast to her inner turmoil,

If she had been at home, she would have pulled the curtains tightly closed, gone to bed, and buried her face in the pillows, with the duvet pulled right up over her head, and stayed there until it was all over. That was the only way she could handle the memories that such an eruption of nature always brought back to her.

But this time there was no possibility of any such escape. There weren't any blinds that she could pull down in order to conceal the dramatic sound and light show playing across the countryside beyond the carriage window. She didn't even have a book or a magazine to distract her. She could only stay in her seat and close her eyes to try and blot out the worst of the tempest, trying not to flinch when the thunder roared.

'Excuse me, dear.'

Jenna jumped, her eyes flying wide open, as a gentle hand was laid on her arm. The woman in the seat opposite was leaning forward, her eyes dark with concern.

'You look very pale. Are you all right?'

'Oh—yes.' Forcing herself to smile, Jenna tried to inject some credibility into her words. 'Just tired. It's been—a long day. Perhaps I just need a cup of coffee to perk me up.'

But this was nothing that a hot drink or a quick nap would cure, she reflected miserably as, her worries eased, the other woman relaxed again. She had been haunted by these fears for five years now. She doubted she would ever be free of them..

All she wanted now was to get home and hide away. Somehow she had to gather the strength to face everyone again in the morning. She had to find some way of coping with the prospect of the wedding on Saturday without breaking apart completely. To do so, she was going to have to put on one of the best acts she had ever managed in her life. Second only to the one she had had to produce five years before.

Then she had been mourning her baby, as well as the way that Connor had walked out of her life.

Under cover of the table between the seats, Jenna's hands clenched into tight fists in her lap, her nails digging sharply into her palms as if that small, acute pain could somehow distract her from the greater, more excruciating one in her heart.

And the worst part of it was that she hadn't been able to share it with anyone.

Joe and Grant had known, of course. There was no way she could have hidden the truth from them. After all, they were the ones who had found her when she had crawled back to the house, soaked through and incoherent with an agony that was a monstrous combination of the physical and mental. It was only then, when she had seen herself in the light, that she had realised that the moisture that soaked her skirt was not just the result of the rain. The darkness of the night had hidden from her the appalling truth—that she was miscarrying her baby.

Grant had taken charge. He had driven her to hospital himself, handling the details that she'd been beyond even being aware of, lost in a world of clawing pain and deepest grief. And it had been Grant who, when she had finally recovered enough to tell him the whole story, had impressed on her the need to keep things secret.

'We'll keep this between ourselves, Jenny love,' he had said, holding her hand as he sat beside her hospital bed. 'It'll be our secret. No one else need know, not even Mum and Dad. From what I've heard Harding's left town and won't be coming back, so you'll never have to face him again. It would be best to put it all behind you and start again.'

And because she'd been so desperately low, completely unable to cope with any more trauma, Jenna had agreed. There had been such a wonderful sense of relief at the thought of just giving up, of handing the whole situation over to her big brother and letting him take charge, that she had trusted him completely.

Grant was never the push-over you believed him to be.

From some bleak, dark corner of her mind Connor's words came back to haunt her, bringing a whimper of distress to her lips.

'Attention please! Attention please!' A disembodied voice on the train's announcement system dragged her back to the present. 'Due to unforeseen circumstances, this train will terminate here. We apologise to all...'

'What?'

Staring round her in dismay and confusion, Jenna caught the eye of the woman who had spoken to her earlier.

'It seems this is as far as we go, love. It's a real bind, isn't it?'

'But what's happening? I didn't hear...'

'The weather's causing problems, apparently.' The older woman shook her head resignedly. 'It seems the storm's resulted in some sort of a landslide on the Greenford line. Lucky for me I wasn't going any further.'

'But I was!'

'Not on this train, you're not. In fact, I doubt if any train'll get through to Greenford before tomorrow evening at the earliest. It looks like you're going to have to make alternative arrangements.'

Numb with shock, Jenna followed everyone else off the train and onto the platform. Once outside, and away from the protective cover of the railway carriage, the force of the storm seemed even worse than before. The thunder crashed deafeningly, almost directly overhead, brilliant lightning snaked across the sky, and the ferocious wind carried the driving rain straight into her face. Struggling with the fear that threatened to paralyse her thought processes, Jenna huddled into the inadequate protection of her linen jacket and set off to try to find out just what was happening.

Half an hour later she was on the verge of despair. Her travelling companion's gloomy predictions had been proved to be true. There was no chance of getting to Greenford by train tonight. And the prospect of any other form of transport was slim.

Couldn't she make her own arrangements?

She had tried. She had rung home, hoping that someone could come out in their car to pick her up. But the only response had been the automated voice on the answering machine, telling her that there was no one there to take her call.

There was only one thing left for it. She would have to fork out the exorbitant fare for a taxi back to Greenford. That was if any driver was prepared to agree to go all that way on such an appalling night.

'Oh, please, please, please...' Jenna found she was muttering the word like an incantation under her breath as she headed out to the front of the station. 'Please let there be a taxi.'

There was. Just one. But even as she headed towards it, a heartfelt prayer of thanks on her lips, the figure of another stranded traveller, unseen until now in the shadows, stepped forward and opened the door of the cab. She could only watch in dismay as the taxi swung away from the kerb and sped off into the night.

'What do I do now?'

There was no answer, of course. Instead, as if to prove that Fate really did have it in for her tonight, the storm, which had temporarily retreated to just a bad-tempered growling in the distance, now swung round again and came back on itself, erupting overhead with renewed and even more savage violence.

'Oh, no! Please—*no*!'

The torrential downpour drenched her in seconds, totally destroying the new hairstyle and plastering the sodden strands around her ashen face. The coral suit fared no better, soaking up the rain like a dishcloth until it clung, limp and clammy, to the slender lines of her body.

All her reserves of strength used up, Jenna felt weak, defeated tears well up in her eyes and trickle down her face, blending with the icy drops of rain so that there was no way of knowing which was which.

'Jenna!'

The shout was barely audible through the storm, the wild force of the wind picking it up and carrying it away so that she was sure she had just been imagining things. Either that or her fears had now started to play on her mind, so that she was hearing voices in the keening of the tempest.

'Jenna! Over here, Jenny Wren!'

Now she knew she was fantasising! Only one person ever used that teasing nickname, and she had left Connor far behind in London, where he was probably safe and snug in the luxurious comfort of his...

But then a movement caught her eye. Through the driving rain she saw a tall, dark-haired figure, long black trenchcoat obviously hastily pulled on and still swinging open over a white tee-shirt and jeans, a hand raised to draw her attention.

Blinking hard in disbelief, she tossed the rats' tails of her hair out of her eyes and looked again. He was still there, and coming closer.

'Jenna—come on!' she could hear him clearly now. 'I've got the car here. Let's get you out of this tempest before you drown.'

An unbridled, ecstatic rush of delight swept through Jenna's battered mind, driving away the despair of moments before. She didn't even pause to wonder just how Connor came to be there, or to remember the circumstances in which they had parted earlier. She only knew that she had never been so glad, so relieved, so absolutely overjoyed to see anyone in her whole life. At this moment, Connor seemed like St George, Sir Lancelot, King Arthur, and any other knight on a white horse riding to the rescue all rolled up into one.

Suddenly she was moving again, her steps getting faster and faster as she dashed towards him. In a world where it seemed that everything had conspired against her, Connor was the one fixed point, the one promise of protection, of safety she could see. And so when he opened his arms wide she didn't even pause, but ran straight into them, sobbing with relief as they closed tightly round her.

CHAPTER ELEVEN

'ALL right now?'

Sniffing inelegantly, Jenna could only manage a silent nod in answer to Connor's careful question. She was still trying to collect together her shattered thoughts and adjust to the new situation in which she now found herself.

Her delight at seeing Connor, at the thought that he had come to her rescue, had temporarily driven all other considerations from her mind. But now, safe and protected in the luxurious interior of his car, speeding towards Greenford, rational thought reasserted itself. And the realisations it forced on her were not at all comfortable.

'Much better, thanks,' she managed at last. 'I'm even beginning to dry out a little bit.' She used the excuse of turning her drenched hair towards the warmth of the heater to cover a sudden need to hide her expression from him. 'So, with luck, I soon won't drip all over your expensive leather seats.'

'What's a few water marks between friends?' Connor's voice was gently amused, unsettling Jenna even more. Nervously she pounced on the only uncomplicated topic of conversation she could think of.

'This isn't your BMW!' It was another car entirely, not the one he had driven her down to London in.

'No, it's not.' Connor laughed. 'Do you really think I could have caught the train if I'd driven all the way? I would have had to go like a bat out of hell to do that.'

'Then how...?'

He smiled at her evident confusion. 'One of the bonuses of being a very rich man. I happen to own a helicopter, with a pilot always on standby. Combine that with the marvels of modern communication like mobile phones and...'

'But how did you know I'd even be on the train?'

That smile grew, made his eyes disturbingly warm.

'I know you, Jenna. When you're hurt or in trouble you always run for home and your family. I originally meant to meet every train at Greenford, but then I heard about the landslide and came here.'

'I wasn't *running*!'

She didn't like the idea that he had seen how much she had been hurt and that he might start to guess at the reasons behind it. Reasons she was only just beginning to understand for herself.

'Perhaps you were right to,' Connor stunned her by saying quietly. 'Jenna, I want to explain about my wife.'

Jenna tossed her almost dry hair back, trying to comb out the tangles with fingers that shook noticeably.

'I don't think I want to hear any explanations. Or anything else for that matter.'

'But *I* want you to hear them.'

Without warning, Connor swung the car to the side of the road and slammed on the brakes with such force that she was jolted painfully in her seat.

'Why have you stopped?' She used indignation to hide the nervous tension that was making her skin prickle with a sensation like painful pins and needles. 'It's late and I want to get home. I have an endless list of things I have to do tomorrow.'

'I'm sure you have,' Connor returned, with a distant formality that Jenna found chilling, making her shiver in spite of the warmth in the car. 'But there are things that need to be said, and I'm not driving any further until you've heard them. So I'm sure you'll appreciate that—'

'That the sooner you've had your say, the sooner I'll get home. All right…' Leaning back in her seat, she folded her arms across her chest with a sigh of resignation. 'Fire away. I'm listening—a captive audience in fact.'

In spite of the gathering darkness in the car she could read his mood with almost frightening ease. He hadn't liked her interruption one little bit. And he had liked her flippant tone even less. Well, let him! It didn't go any way towards easing the jagged, uneasy mood she was enduring to know that he felt the same way, but at least a sort of gloomy satisfaction was better than nothing.

'First of all, I want you to know I had no idea that that photo of Lucy was under the bed. I haven't been in the flat for months, and God knows when it actually ended up under there. I couldn't believe the bad luck that meant—'

'I bet you couldn't!' Desperate now to make up the ground she had lost by her reaction to his arrival at the station, Jenna realised that attack was very definitely the best form of defence. 'It really ruined all your sordid little plans, didn't it? You had me right where you wanted, the perfect substitute almost in your bed, and—'

'Jenna, stop it!'

Moving sharply, Connor snapped on the interior light with a suddenness that made her jump like a frightened cat. Turning wide green eyes on the hard, set lines of his face, she subsided into wary silence. The shadows in the car exaggerated the carved cheekbones, the lean planes of his cheeks and the deep, dark pools of his eyes in a way that made her pulse leap in apprehension.

'Just shut up and listen! You were never a substitute for Lucy, *never*...'

'I look just like her!' In spite of her dread of his anger she couldn't keep quiet. 'We might be twins.'

'You don't look like her,' Connor spelt out through gritted teeth. '*She* looks just like *you*. There is a difference.'

'Not from where I'm sitting,' Jenna declared inflexibly. 'And besides, most men go for a certain type...'

'Damn you, Jenna, will you *listen*? Lucy was not a "type", any more than your Graham is my type.'

Suddenly Jenna thought she saw the direction in which his argument was heading, and it wasn't one she was at all keen on pursuing.

'Are you saying that I'm attracted to Graham because he reminds me of you?'

The look Connor turned on her had an unnerving 'if the cap fits' element about it that had her shifting uncomfortably in her seat.

'And I suppose you think I'm marrying him because I still have a thing about you!'

'They say no one ever forgets their first lover.'

'Unfortunately, that's true,' Jenna conceded acidly. 'But not because you were so wonderful that you've stayed in my memory as the standard by which all future relationships are to be measured. On the contrary, I could never forget you because you were—are—the archetypal rat—the sort of man I was determined never, ever to tangle with again!'

Connor's eyes narrowed dangerously, his hands stiffening on the wheel. Above their heads, the rain thundered down on the roof of the car.

'But just now—at the station—you came into my arms…'

'Perhaps I did.'

You *know* you did, a small, reproving voice at the back of her mind put in. You flew into his arms and it felt like coming home, like reaching the perfect haven, the place where you were always truly meant to be. But she would die before she admitted as much to Connor.

'But that wasn't because it was *you*. I was so scared, so stressed out, that I would have been glad to see anyone— anyone at all. If the devil himself had turned up offering help at that moment, I would have flung myself into his arms too.'

Which was obviously not at all what he wanted to hear.

Tough, Jenna told him in the privacy of her own thoughts. What did you think? That I would declare undying love, tell you you had stolen my heart years ago and I had never wanted it back? That I couldn't live without you, and no matter how badly you treat me, I will always feel the same? No way!

But even as she formed the thoughts, that unwanted, intrusive little voice inside her head changed its tune and started to challenge the sincerity of what she was feeling.

'And besides—' in an effort to drown out the awkward and uncomfortable questions, she adopted what she hoped was a convincingly fiery tone '—any comfort you could offer me is now at least five years too late.'

'Five years,' Connor echoed, a new and very worrying intonation shading his words. 'Is that what all this is about? There was a storm that night...'

Jenna's mind went blank in shock. She had never dreamed that he would remember. That he would home in on the reason for her fear and go straight to the heart of things without even missing a beat.

'Is that why you're so terrified of thunderstorms?'

'Exactly what night are we talking about?' Jenna hedged desperately, then flinched fearfully as Connor's hand, clenched into a fist, came down hard on the side of the steering wheel.

'You know very well just what night I mean! The night you rang me up and left me an ultimatum on the answer-machine.'

Jenna couldn't understand the cold fury in his eyes, the tension that made a muscle jerk in his jaw.

'It wasn't an ultimatum!' she cried desperately, her voice shaking with the echoes of remembered pain. 'I was frantic. I couldn't think what else to do! You'd just walked away...abandoned me and the baby.'

'No, I didn't!' Connor shook his dark head in violent negation.

'I told you I was pregnant and—'

'Oh, yes, you told me, all right. You were pure Kenyon through and through, telling me just how things were going to be—what you wanted me to do.' His beautiful mouth twisted into a wry grimace. 'I don't take too well to being ordered around, so I said give me till the end of the week. I didn't even manage that. I came back—'

'I don't believe you!'

'I *came back*,' Connor insisted, every word a savage reproach. 'I came to the house, but you weren't there. Instead, I had the misfortune to come face to face with your big brother.'

'Grant?'

'Grant,' he confirmed harshly. 'He told me in no uncertain terms that you didn't want to see me ever again.'

'Now I know you're lying! Grant wouldn't have said anything because he didn't know about us—then.'

'Are you sure?'

'Absolu…' Jenna began, but then, looking into his face, her confidence evaporated and she couldn't finish.

She would have sworn that Grant hadn't known a thing about her relationship with Connor, that she had been careful enough and clever enough to conceal it from everyone in her family. But that dreadful time, when she had come home distraught and bleeding, her brother hadn't needed any explanations. She hadn't told him whose baby she had lost, but he had known.

'That bastard Harding!' he had raved. 'When I get my hands on him, I'll kill him!'

It was a frightening experience to feel the well-shored convictions and prejudices that she had held so securely over the past five years begin to come apart at the seams. Everything she had thought about Connor in that time had been built on those convictions. If they crumbled, came crashing down at her feet, what would she put in their place?

'That time when I rang you…'

He hadn't been at his mother's house. Instead, she had heard the heartless, automated voice on the answer-machine, telling her to leave her message after the signal. Just the thought of Connor playing the recording back, listening to her when he could be bothered to, possibly even wiping the tape as soon as he realised who had phoned, had been enough to stiffen her voice, turning what she had to say into an emotionless, coldly enunciated statement.

'Connor, we can't leave things as they are; we have to talk. Meet me tonight in the old bandstand in the park—around eight? I'll wait for you there.'

She had been about to put the phone down when the fear that he might just not care enough even to turn up had pushed her to add hastily, 'If you don't come, I'll take that as meaning you want nothing to do with me. In that case I shall have to deal with things my own way. I'm sure you don't want to push me into doing something you might regret.'

'You tell me about that time,' Connor instructed coldly now.

'There's very little to tell.' The words came slowly, reluctantly, no life in her voice. 'I went to the park, as I'd said. I waited...'

She had been so sure he would come. Convinced that, with the shock lessened, his temper cooled, he would be there to take her in his arms, tell her that he loved her, that everything would be all right now.

Instead she had waited and waited. Almost an hour had gone by before she heard the first rumble of thunder, seen the flash of lightning, but still she had stayed. And then the rain had begun.

'I thought that perhaps you'd been out of town, that you might not get the message until late, so I hung on. I felt a bit strange—faint and dizzy—but I put that down to the fact that I hadn't been able to eat anything—nerves, I suppose.'

In her lap, Jenna's hands clenched over each other, nails digging into tender flesh as she twisted them round and round. From his seat, Connor simply watched her, silent and still, his eyes never leaving her pale, harrowed face.

'I put the pain down to the same explanation, too.'

She was speaking more quickly now, anxious to get the whole appalling story out into the open. But her tone was that of a well-programmed robot, flat, dead, unchanging. She was incapable of injecting any emotion into her account. *That* was all in her mind, and if she let it seep into what she was saying she would break apart completely, totally unable to go on.

'Well, it wasn't a pain at first, more a queasiness—like indigestion, or that hollow feeling you get when you're really hungry. And I was so used to feeling sick, with the…the…' For the first time she faltered, swallowing down the knot of tears that clogged her throat. 'With the baby, that I just ignored it.'

She'd refused to let it register; refused to let her mind even acknowledge what was happening. In some foolish way she had managed to convince herself that if she didn't admit to what she felt then it wouldn't be true. It would all be just in her imagination, no foundation in fact.

'But then it got worse. It—it *hurt*.'

Her mouth contorted as she struggled to keep speaking. It was just as she had feared. She had tried to lock those nightmare memories away, but they had always been there, just under the surface, the wounds only barely healed. Even just remembering was like gouging open those fragile scars, making them bleed anew.

'But I wanted to wait for you…'

At her side, Connor made a violent, uncontrolled sound in his throat that brought her head swinging round to him. His eyes were just black, fathomless pools in a face so drawn it was as if there was no flesh on his bones.

'I was so sure you would come. I waited and waited, but then I felt so ill I knew I just had to get home.'

Jenna's hands went up before her face, covering her eyes. Recalling this, the worst of it, she found it easier to speak from behind their concealing protection, her thoughts projected inward. Her heart was racing with remembered panic, the desperate conviction that something had been very, very wrong.

'It seemed to take for ever, and all the time the storm raged—I was terrified the lightning might strike me, or the wind blow me over and I'd never get up again. I don't know how I got home, but I did—and Grant and Joe were there—

and they took one look at me and—and that was when I realised...when I saw...'

'*Jenna!*' Her name was a hoarse sound of horror, and her concealing hands were dragged from her eyes, forcing her to look into Connor's ravaged face. 'Are you telling me that—that you...?'

It was so unusual to see Connor—articulate, confident, self-assured Connor—stumbling over his words, struggling to find the right thing to say, that Jenna actually laughed. But there was no trace of humour in her response. It was only a weak, shaky thread of sound, simply an expression of her amazement at this change in him.

'That you miscarried the baby? That you didn't—?'

'Didn't what, Connor?' Jenna whispered, frowning in bewilderment when he broke off again. 'Didn't...?'

She had thought she'd endured every horror it was possible to face, experienced the worst possible pain, but suddenly there was a new one staring her right in the face. It seemed she hadn't quite scraped the bottom of the barrel—not until now.

'You can't mean...'

But he *had* meant it. It was written on his face, etched into the lines around his eyes and mouth. Now at last she understood the vicious contempt that she had seen in him before, the look of pure loathing he had turned on her from the first. And as the full impact of what he was implying sank in a roaring red haze of fury swept the anguish from her thoughts.

'You bastard! You really thought I'd had an abortion! That I'd killed our baby! How could you...?'

Ignoring the restriction of her seat belt, she launched herself at him, her cry of fury and pain wild as the howl of some feral animal. Half blinded by the tears that poured down her cheeks, she let fly with her fists, as if by physical violence she could ease the pain in her heart.

The frantic, unseeing blows landed on his arm, his chest, one might even have struck his face if hadn't jerked his head back instinctively. As it was, her hand skimmed his cheek, a nail catching the skin and leaving an ugly scratch.

'How could you…? How *could* you?'

The words became an incoherent litany of despair, repeated over and over because a purely physical reaction was not enough. She had to say something, needed to use as many means as possible of expressing the way she felt.

'How *could* you!'

'Very easily,' Connor put in quietly, stunning her into stopping dead, her fists still half raised. 'Think about it, Jenny Wren…' This time there was no affection, no warmth at all in the old nickname. 'When you told me you were pregnant you gave me just two options…'

Holding up one hand between them, he marked off his points on the long, tanned fingers.

'Option one: marriage as soon as possible, in order not to offend the delicate Kenyon sensibilities. Option two: termination. There was nothing in between. No possibility of compromise. It was either/or—just that. So, when you seemed to believe that option one had fallen through, what else was I to think you'd be likely to do? Especially when you gave me that ultimatum.'

'…I shall have to deal with things my own way.' Jenna could hear her own voice saying the words on that fateful night. 'I'm sure you don't want to push me into doing something you might regret.'

Slowly, limply, her hands fell to her sides; she no longer had the strength to hold them up. Her brain felt as battered and bruised as if she had just been in a boxing ring with the heavyweight champion of the world.

'I meant that I would have to tell my parents I was having your baby but that you had shrugged off all responsibility for it. I was sure you wouldn't want me to do that, not knowing how my father felt about you.'

Connor's grim expression told its own story.

'I would most definitely *not* have wanted you to do that.'

Jenna had had as much as she could take. She felt numb,

bone-weary, exhausted by all that had happened since she had left Greenford with Connor that morning. It felt as if she had lived through a hundred lifetimes since then, not just a few short hours.

'Do you think we could go home now?' she asked, in a voice that was drained of all feeling.

'Sure.'

Connor switched off the light and moved to start the car. A few seconds later they were back on the road, heading once more for Greenford.

Jenna could only be thankful that the darkness that had descended as they talked now hid her face and the emotions she couldn't have concealed if she tried. But she was past trying, and could only sit in silence, letting her thoughts free to face the truth at last.

'Do you think we could go home now?' she had said, and it was impossible not to remember the moment at the station when she had flung herself into Connor's arms and believed herself truly at home at last. But that feeling had only been a delusion, temporary, fleeting as a perfect rainbow and just as impossible to hold onto.

Never once had Connor expressed any emotion towards her other than purely physical desire, the blazing, hungry passion that he found impossible to hide. And because of that his arms were not the true haven, the sanctuary she had dreamed of. That could only come from knowing that you were loved and loving deeply in return.

There. Now she'd done it. She had finally let that persistent nagging little voice have its say and had acknowledged the truth of its assertions, if only to herself. She had tried to convince herself that she hated Connor, but that had been a lost cause from the start. His return to Greenford, his attempts to revive the sexual affair they had had in the past, could never have affected her as strongly as they had if hatred had been truly what she felt.

And if she had had any doubts, then the anguish she had felt at seeing that photograph of Lucy had burned them all away, like tinder-dry grass in the path of a blazing forest fire. That pain had brought the truth right out into the open, slapped her hard in the face with it so that there was no possibility of ever retreating into the refuge of self-deception again.

She loved Connor. It was as simple and as devastating as that. She had always loved him, still loved him, and would always love him, and there wasn't a thing in the world she could do to change it.

It was as the car finally pulled up outside her parents' home that a new and vital question formed in her mind, demanding an answer with an urgency that drove away all other considerations.

'Can—can I ask you a question?' she asked as the sound of the engine stilled.

'Fire away.'

'Did…?' The words caught in the knot of feelings blocking her throat and she had to force them out in a clumsy rush. 'Our baby—when I told you I was pregnant, did you ever really want our baby then?'

Connor drew in a deep breath on a long, ragged sigh and pushed both hands into the midnight darkness of his hair, pressing his fingers into the bones of his skull.

'If I'm honest, no,' he said at last, staring out into the darkness beyond the windscreen. 'I wasn't ready for the responsibility of being a father then.'

Or for anything else, Jenna reflected drearily. He might have come back to her that first time, and Grant had intervened, but never once had he said that he had come to offer marriage, or to tell her that he loved her. He had simply planned on discussing what he had termed their 'options', and having tried once he had never come again.

So if she was tempted to wonder what might have happened if things had been different, if Grant had never realised what was going on and hadn't told Connor that she didn't want to see him, now she had her answer.

Nothing would have changed. Connor would never have

made any sort of commitment to her; he valued his freedom and his career too highly for that. He might have offered her some form of financial support, perhaps even wanted to see the baby once in a while, but that was all.

And she would still have lost the baby. The doctors had told her that the miscarriage hadn't been the stress of the storm, or the result of getting soaked to the skin, but one of those accidents of nature that no one could predict or prevent. So it would have happened anyway, and when it had Connor would have walked away from her just the same. He would have gone, never looking back, knowing only a sense of relief that he had emerged with his precious freedom unscathed, his proud ambition unencumbered by the restrictions of fatherhood.

And she would have been left alone, breaking her heart for loving him and knowing that he would never return that love.

'Jenna...' Connor had turned to her, one lean hand covering both of her own where they lay loosely in her lap. 'I am truly sorry about what happened to you and the baby.'

It was too much. To hear him declare that he was *sorry* that she had lost a baby he had just admitted he had never even wanted was more than she could bear.

'You *hypocrite*! You monstrous, hateful, total fraud! Don't come to me with your sorries now! Five years ago, I might have given you a hearing—I was a lot younger, and *much* more foolish then! But not now!'

'Jenny...' Connor tried to put in, but the sound of that once affectionate name on his lying lips pushed her right over the edge.

'No! I don't want to listen to another word from you ever again! Never! In fact, if I ever see you again in the whole of my life it will be way too soon.'

Frantically she fumbled with the fastening of her seat belt, desperate to be out of the car and away from him. To her distress the catch eluded her, and she flung her hands in the air, almost screaming in frustration.

'Let me out of here!'

His expression closed and tight, dark eyes shuttered against her, Connor reached out and freed the offending clasp with an efficient economy of movement that was in stark contrast to her own flustered impotence. But then, as she flung open the door and tried to clamber out, he lunged forward and clamped powerful fingers around her wrist, holding her prisoner.

'Just tell me one thing,' he grated, his eyes drained of all colour in the moonlight, making her think fearfully of a hunting animal's. 'This bloody wedding on Saturday—is it still going ahead?'

The truth was that it hadn't even crossed her mind. Just for a second, the realisation made her heart skip a beat, leaving her frighteningly vulnerable to his attack. But then, swiftly, she recollected herself and lifted her chin, green eyes blazing into his in open defiance.

'Of course!' she flung into his rigid face. 'Of course the wedding will still go ahead. Two o'clock, Saturday—the parish church. Do you really think that anything that's happened will change that?'

Connor dropped her hand as swiftly and violently as if he had just discovered that she had some appalling disease and feared she would contaminate him. He made no further move to stop her as she scrambled out of the car, unable to get away quickly enough.

'Just one more thing, Jenna,' he tossed after her, his low voice darkened by a terrible savagery that was lethal to what was left of her self-control. 'Don't go flinging accusations of hypocrisy around unless you're totally confident that your own conscience is clear enough to bear close scrutiny. I mean, be honest, we may not actually have made love tonight—not physically. But in your mind and in your heart you were as unfaithful to Graham as it's possible for a woman to be!'

CHAPTER TWELVE

How many times had she visited this hotel in the past few weeks? Jenna was forced to wonder as she paused just inside the foyer of the George to draw breath and nerve herself to go on. A dozen or so? Certainly she seemed to have been here at least once every day, sometimes more, since the countdown to the big day of the wedding had begun in earnest.

But this time had to be the hardest, the one she found most difficult to handle. Just the thought of what was ahead of her turned her legs to water, made her heart shudder fearfully.

She had to struggle to make herself use the lift. Vivid images of the time she had spent in it with Connor, just four days before, returned to plague her as she was whisked swiftly upstairs, making her groan aloud. She had to close her eyes so as not to see her own reflection in the glassed walls, the hectic colour in her otherwise deathly pale cheeks that flared wildly at just the thought of the way she had felt then.

Connor hadn't checked out of the hotel. Discreet enquiries at the reception desk had made sure that he was still staying in the hotel, although no one had seen hide nor hair of him over the past forty-eight hours.

If the receptionist on duty had thought that almost eight o'clock on a Friday night was an unusual hour to check on the last-minute details for tomorrow's reception, she hadn't said anything. After all, no one wanted to risk any possibility of any spanners in the works of what would be potentially the most glamorous, and certainly, for the hotel, the most profitable society wedding for years.

Connor must have heard the lift reach the ninth floor, because she had barely had time to square her slim shoulders under the dark green cotton dress, draw a deep nervous breath and tap lightly at the door before it was yanked open.

'Well, well, if it isn't Saturday's bride.'

Connor's deep voice was rich with a fiendish mockery as he lounged in the open doorway, a crumpled black shirt hanging open over the width of his tanned chest, his hands pushed deep into the pockets of scruffy denim jeans.

'Or perhaps I should say tomorrow's bride, seeing as there's what...? Less than twenty hours to go to the big event?'

Clamping her mouth tight shut on the gasp of distress his cynical greeting had almost drawn from her, Jenna eyed him warily. The dark brown hair was rough and dishevelled, far from its usual sleek perfection, and he obviously hadn't shaved at all today. Those stunning sapphire eyes looked strangely faded, as if something had leached away their brilliant colour, leaving them just a pale shadow of their former beauty.

'Have you been drinking?' she asked suspiciously.

'If I have, that's my concern and mine alone,' Connor flung back aggressively. 'What I do in the privacy of my own life is none of your business, so I'll thank you to leave me very much alone in the future.'

Two 'alones' in just a couple of sentences, Jenna registered worriedly. And his voice had a bruised quality that she had never heard in it before. Just what was going on behind those carefully shuttered eyes, in the thoughts he was so obviously determined to conceal from her?

'Which reminds me,' Connor went on, with the air of a man who had just made a discovery of major importance. 'Shouldn't you be at your hen night, or whatever you choose to call it? No...?' As she shook her dark head in response. 'Well, then, am I to assume that the blushing bridegroom is safely ensconced in some public house indulging in a riotously drunken stag night?'

'Graham...' Her voice cracked on the name, sounding rough and hoarse. 'Graham doesn't approve of such things. He's...he's at home...'

Hastily she clamped her mouth shut on the careless words that had the potential to toss a lighted match into the already explosive situation.

'That figures.' The cynicism became more pronounced, dangerously so. 'I'm sure he's saving himself for the delights of the wedding night to come. So why are you here, my sweet Jenny Wren? To what do I owe the pleasure of your delightful company?'

That was the question she had known he was bound to ask. The million-dollar question that she still hadn't prepared a satisfactory answer to.

'I—I wanted to talk...'

'But I don't. Goodnight.'

It was brusquely dismissive, and he would have shut the door quite cold-bloodedly in her face if she hadn't moved forward hastily and put out a hand to prevent it.

'Connor, *please*... Grant said I should talk to you.'

That stopped him dead. The blue eyes went to her face, scrutinising her fine-boned features with an intensity that made her feel as if her skin might actually scorch where his gaze rested.

'*Grant!* What the hell has your brother got to do with this?'

'I think you know. Or at least you can begin to guess.' The way that cold-eyed assessment changed to an odd vulnerability told her that she was on the right track, encouraging her to press home her advantage. 'But if you let me in, I'll explain everything.'

For the space of a couple of decidedly jerky heartbeats, he eyed her in silence, reluctance to agree to anything she said stamped clearly on the strong features. But then, just as she drew breath to nerve herself to plead with him further, he obviously changed his mind and let the door swing open, one strong hand sketching a mocking gesture of invitation.

'Be my guest,' he said, stepping back to let her move past him.

The sitting room she walked into was large, and luxuriously furnished in tones of burgundy and cream, but Jenna was too much on edge to take in her surroundings fully.

Behind her, Connor strode across the room, kicked the bedroom door shut and then leaned back against it, arms folded firmly across his chest, eyes coldly assessing.

'Do you want to sit down?' It was a million miles away from a polite invitation. Guaranteed to ensure she did not feel at home.

'O-only if you do.'

She didn't want to find herself with Connor towering way above her. She felt vulnerable enough already, and his impressive height and strength had always given him an unfair advantage. Connor dismissed her stumbling words with an imperious wave of one hand.

'I don't think that will be necessary. Will this take long? Grant?' he prompted harshly when she licked her lips uncertainly, unable to find the courage to begin. 'You had some message from your brother, I believe.'

'Not from Grant, *about* him.' Her voice was too high-pitched and squeaky. Clearing her throat nervously, she forced it down an octave. 'As you know, we had a family party last night. G-Grant brought his wife and his two little girls. He'd heard you were in town.'

'Then I suppose I should count myself lucky I'm still alive.' The bleak flippancy made her wince painfully. 'As I remember it, your brother had a one-man crusade of hatred against me.'

'I know. He admitted that. He also acknowledged that he'd not been fair to you in the past.'

'Big of him.' But in spite of himself Connor was obviously intrigued. He was actually listening, blue eyes meeting green properly for the first time, that defensive armour of aggression easing just a little bit. 'And what brought about this admission?'

'We were talking...'

Jenna was picturing the scene as she spoke. The room crowded with her family and Graham's. Her brothers back in full force for the first time in years, all with their wives and the next generation of young Kenyons, her nephews and nieces.

The formal meal had been over, and everyone had broken up into small groups, chatting amongst themselves. She had been sitting on the window seat that filled the wide arch of the bay window, watching quietly, when Grant had lowered his strong frame onto the seat beside her.

'So, how's my little sister keeping these days?' he enquired. 'You know, we don't see enough of you up here. But city life obviously suits you. That dress is stunning...' A wave of his hand indicated the simple cream satin dress she wore. 'Elegant and sophisticated. In fact both the Kenyon girls are looking spectacularly beautiful tonight.'

Jenna's eyes went to where Susie, her softer colouring enhanced by the pale green of her lacy shift, was talking animatedly to Graham on the other side of the room.

'Mmm.'

It was all she could manage. Ever since she had left Connor the previous night her mind had been in turmoil, her emotions swinging this way and that until she had felt like weeping in panic and despair. She envied her sister her simple, uncomplicated delight in Graham's company that was in such stark contrast to her own impossibly tangled feelings.

Beside her, Grant cleared his throat awkwardly.

'What is it, Jen? You're as jumpy as a cat on a hot tin roof tonight. Something's obviously troubling you. Is Connor Harding behind all this?'

The emotive sound of the name she had tried so hard and so unsuccessfully to keep from her thoughts had Jenna spinning round, eyes wide and brilliant as emeralds above suddenly colourless cheeks.

'I heard he was in town,' her brother said, and to Jenna's astonishment he actually looked uncharacteristically embarrassed. 'As a matter of fact, I was thinking of going to see him, but I wanted to check with you first.'

'See him?' Jenna croaked. 'What on earth for?'

'Well, I have to admit that my conscience isn't exactly clear where Connor's concerned. All right, I behaved like a damn fool towards him sometimes. If you want the truth, I was jealous as hell—of his looks, his talent, his success with women. He made me feel second-best, and I didn't like that. But it's what I might have done to you as a result that worries me.'

'Done to me! Grant, what are you talking about?'

Her brother shifted uncomfortably in his seat. 'That time when he got you pregnant...'

'I know that you told him I didn't want to see him,' Jenna said carefully, when he obviously found it difficult to continue. 'Connor and I have—talked. I didn't know you'd found out about us seeing each other.'

'A friend of Joe's spotted you together in York and told us about it. And was that all that Connor said? He didn't give you the rest of the sordid details? Obviously not,' Grant answered his own question when she turned a confused and puzzled glance on him.

'What sordid details?' Jenna's head was spinning, the noise of the others in the room sounding as if it was reaching her down a long, echoing tunnel. 'Grant, you must tell me!'

'I had to drag it out of him,' she told Connor now. 'But he admitted it all in the end.'

'All?' Connor's voice sounded thick and rough. He raised a finger to the small silvery scar above his left eyebrow, rubbing at it as if it was troubling him.

'Connor, why didn't you tell me that you came back a second time?' It was a question, a commiseration and a reproach all rolled into one. 'Why didn't you tell me that you were there on the night of the storm—the night I lost the baby?'

Her answer was there in his face as soon as she asked the question. It was clear from the way he flinched away from her words, heavy lids swiftly hooding his eyes from her, but not before she had caught the betraying sheen in them.

He was *hurting* about this—about the baby, she realised, with a shock that was like a blow to her heart. That night in his car he had been almost as devastated as she had to learn of her miscarriage, particularly after believing for five long years that she had deliberately aborted their child. Then she had been too caught up in her own pain to see what was happening to him. She had let her bitterness blind her. But now her eyes were wide open.

'I was ashamed.' He wouldn't look at her, but stared fixedly at the carpet.

'Ashamed?' It was the last thing she had expected.

He had taken all the abuse, all the vile things she had spat at him, even let her attack him physically, when all the time he could have crushed her anger, her violent censure, with a single sentence. Instead he had stayed silent, letting her do her worst.

'But why?'

Connor sighed heavily, his throat working as he swallowed hard.

'I let you down,' he said flatly. 'I wasn't there when you needed me. I was out when you rang and I didn't get the message you left until late.'

The blue eyes flicked up swiftly, locked with her shocked green ones for just a second, then dropped to the floor again, studying the toes of his shoes with a fierce concentration.

'The truth is that I was in the pub, still trying to come to terms with the fact that you didn't even want me as a father to your child any more. That you'd slammed the door in my face—using your brother as go-between, of course.'

'You were drunk?'

A faint smile touched his lips, but it was bleak and desolate, only the very blackest amusement in it.

'Out of my head with it, but I pretty soon sobered up when I got back and found your message waiting for me. Of course I was in no fit state to drive, so I ran.' His mouth twisted, his brief crack of laughter harsh as the lash of a whip. 'I must have looked as if all the devils in hell were after me, but by the time I reached the park you'd already gone.'

'You went to the park too?'

Grant hadn't known that. Last night he'd only told her that Connor had arrived, breathless, dishevelled and drenched by the rain, demanding to see her no matter how late it was.

'When I got to your house, only Grant was still up. He said you weren't there, that you'd never be there for me again. He said you were in hospital that—that...'

'He told me what he said,' Jenna put in softly when Connor's voice failed him.

'I hated him for what he'd done to you,' Grant had admitted. 'I wanted to hurt him as you were hurting. I really wanted to kill him. And, most of all, I wanted to make sure that he never came near you ever again. So I told him that I knew about the baby and I—I implied that you'd gone into hospital to have a termination. I said that at least you had had the sense to get rid of his little bastard before it grew up to be a real problem to us all. And then I hit him.'

Moving swiftly to Connor's side, Jenna caught hold of the restless hand that was still fretting at the scar on his forehead. Her green eyes deep and shadowed as a mossy pool, she traced the fine line with gentle fingertips.

'Grant did that to you.' It was a statement, not a question. A statement filled with deep-felt regret.

Because Connor hadn't fought back. Grant had told her

that, shaking his head in bemused remorse. He had found it hard to believe in Connor's reaction even now, looking back with the benefit of hindsight after the five intervening years.

Grant hadn't been able to understand. But after hearing Connor's rawly voiced, 'I was ashamed...I let you down,' Jenna thought that she did. She could see how he would have blamed himself for the desperate action he thought she had taken, and that he would have seen Grant's reaction as justified, meting out a harsh but necessary penance for his sins.

This was what Grant had had on his conscience. What she now had on hers.

'But you said you didn't want the baby.'

Connor's sigh seemed to come from the depths of his soul.

'I paid you the compliment of being completely straight. A baby was the last thing I wanted—at first. Fatherhood wasn't at all how I'd mapped out the next stage of my life, particularly not when I thought we'd taken precautions against it. But the more I thought about it, the more I warmed to the idea. In the end I realised that I'd got it all wrong. That my restlessness was not because I needed more material success in my life, but quite the opposite. I needed someone to love.'

His head came up sharply, blue eyes blazing into hers.

'And I would have loved that baby with all my heart.'

Instead of which, he'd been led to believe that she had deliberately terminated the pregnancy.

'Connor,' she whispered. 'I'm sorry. So sorry.'

Once more his mouth quirked up at the corners, this time with a trace of more genuine humour.

'I rather think that's my line.'

As if he couldn't help himself, he turned his head into her hand, pressing a swift, warm kiss on the palm that still lay against his cheek.

Jenna's heart jolted sharply, stopped dead for a couple

of breathless seconds. Then just as suddenly the blood was singing through her veins, carrying a wild, fizzing heat throughout her body, but most particularly towards her heart.

Impulsively standing on tiptoe, one hand resting on the strength of his chest to support herself, she took her fingers away from the small scar and replaced them with her lips. Then she let her mouth follow the black line of his brow down, past the corner of his eye, along the slash of his cheekbone.

Connor had frozen at the first touch of her lips. He remained totally still, barely breathing, as she let the trail of soft kisses take her lower, lower, until she was less than an inch away from his mouth.

Then he closed his eyes, drew in a deep, ragged sigh that told its own story. Beneath her hand his heart was pounding, hard and fast, betraying the truth of his response, but still he was holding his breath, holding himself in, using every ounce of control he possessed not to react. The sort of inhuman, ruthless control Jenna knew only too well he was capable of, but which she now wanted to destroy once and for all.

'If you stop now...' His voice was cracked and rasping, as if he hadn't used it for a very long time. 'Then I might just be able to let you go.'

Jenna's pulse was like thunder in her head. But *this* storm didn't frighten her. She welcomed it gladly, wanted it to build and build.

'And what if I don't want you to let me go?' she asked softly, the words catching in her throat as those sapphire eyes suddenly flew open again, blue fire blazing straight into hers. 'What if want you to hold me and kiss me and—?'

He didn't let her finish. With a thick groan of surrender deep in his throat he reached for her, twisting her in his hold until she was bent backwards over the supporting strength of one arm. The kisses he rained on her face, crushed against her mouth, were frantic, hungry, desperate. That control she so detested was gone at last, broken— destroyed, it seemed, for good.

And she was kissing him back, matching his hunger with her own, meeting the force of his need more than halfway. It was so easy now to let her own sense of restraint dissipate completely, swept away on a burning tide of passion that erased any taint of the past, leaving a whole, new brilliant future lying ahead of them like a promise.

With that restraint gone, all that was left was the wild, frenzied need they had for each other. The potent force that had them clinging, straining, body to body, hands moulding, caressing, arousing. The rasp of their breathing, as out of control as the rest of their senses, was the only sound in the silence of the room.

Each of them played an equal part in dispensing with the unwanted restriction of clothing, fingers fumbling in urgent haste as they wrenched fastenings open, tossing aside the discarded items. And all the time their mouths were locked together, hot and moist, tongues tangling in a wild dance of intimacy.

Jenna would never be sure whether Connor actually lowered her to the thickness of the carpet or whether the sheer force of their kisses, the need of their bodies, toppled them as if they had been swept off their feet by the power of a tidal wave. She only knew she went with him willingly, that it was her own arms that drew him down on top of her, holding him close when he tensed suddenly, a glimmer of rational thought sliding into his mind.

'Jenna...' Her name was a breathless, shaken sound, threaded through with an edge of disbelieving laughter. 'This is crazy! There are two perfectly comfortable beds...'

The words were swallowed back down his throat as Jenna stopped his mouth with her own.

'We've no time for beds,' she assured him against his lips. 'This is what I want. What I need.'

And she arched her body against his, glorying in the

powerful masculine desire she could feel, heated steel and velvet, against her thighs.

What she was feeling was too strong, too primitive to allow for a decorous retiring to the civilised comfort of a bed. She felt wild and wanton, exhilarated by the erotic power of her own responses and the way that Connor matched her neediness at every stage.

The burn of his mouth on her breasts had her crying aloud in delight, eyes closing tight to allow her to concentrate solely on the sharply exquisite sensations that fierce tugging could produce. But then the touch of his hands at the most intimate core of her body brought them open wide again, to stare blankly, sightlessly above her, a moan of carnal hunger escaping her shattered control.

Fingers clenching in the dark silk of his hair, she dragged his head up towards her own, small white teeth worrying at the soft lobe of his ear.

'Come into me now, Connor,' she breathed against his skin. 'I want to feel you there, know you completely.'

His only verbal response was a choked, incoherent sound, his command of himself too far gone to allow for any more articulate reaction. But his body spoke for him, thrusting into her with a force and strength that splintered her sense of reality, bringing stormy, unrestrained tears of delight to her eyes.

And after that she too was beyond speech, could only feel. She could do nothing but let the pulsing, fiery crescendo of ecstasy they created between them grow and grow, carrying them higher and higher until in a brilliant explosion of stars they both reached the shuddering, soul-wrenching peak.

CHAPTER THIRTEEN

THE brilliant light of the sun blazing through the window with the promise of another perfect summer day dragged Jenna unwillingly from sleep.

They hadn't bothered to draw the curtains last night. If the truth were told, the thought had never even crossed their minds. They had barely even bothered with a bed in the end.

But at some point, late into the long, passion-filled hours, Connor had roused himself enough to lift her from where she lay, exhausted and, temporarily at least, satiated on the pleasures of lovemaking, and carried her into his bedroom.

The cool touch of the bedclothes, the change in position, had been enough to wake her. Eyes still closed, she had reached for him hungrily, her soft body coiling round the hard strength of his, inviting his caresses once more. An invitation he had had no hesitation in taking up enthusiastically.

Smiling softly, Jenna yawned, stretching languorously, glorying in the faint aches and tender spots all over her body that told of the fierce ardour of Connor's lovemaking. She would let him sleep for a little while longer, and then...

But suddenly recognition of a certain quality about the light had her sitting up hastily, shock clearing all remaining traces of sleep dullness from her mind. A swift glance at Connor's watch, discarded on the bedside table, confirmed her fears, setting her heart racing in disturbed reaction.

It was Saturday morning. The day of the wedding.

Already her mother and Susie would be up, would knock on the door of her bedroom, wanting to share the first moments of this special day. If she wasn't there then they and all the rest of her family would be frantic, tearing their hair in panic.

'Connor...'

Reluctantly her gaze went to where he lay, dead to the world, his long, tanned body entangled in a coil of sheets. The deep brown hair had fallen forward over his face, giving him a disturbingly boyish look, one that was enhanced by the impossibly luxurious thickness of the rich black lashes lying in an arc above the carved line of his cheekbones.

But the dark shadowing of his strong jaw was all man, no trace of softness there. As she knew to her cost, Jenna reflected ruefully, smoothing a hand over the delicate skin of her face, which still bore the red marks inflicted on it by the roughness of a day's growth of beard.

'Connor...'she tried again, still getting no response.

It was as she lifted her hand to shake him into some degree of wakefulness that a new and uncomfortable thought invaded her contentment. One that had her frowning in disturbed uncertainty, something of her elated mood evaporating swiftly as she faced the one flaw that had marred the perfection of the night.

It had been as weariness finally claimed them for the last time, forcing on them a sleep they could no longer resist, that Connor had pulled her close against him, curving his long body around the line of her back, one heavy arm clamping her possessively into place. Sighing his drowsy satisfaction in her ear, he had laughed softly, the sound disturbingly triumphant.

'I knew I wouldn't need five days to convince you Graham was wrong for you—to get you away from him.'

Sleep had claimed her before she'd had time to fully register the implications of the purred comment, but now, in the brutal light of day, it came back to haunt her with a force that made her shudder in sudden fear.

She had taken a great deal for granted last night. Connor's reaction had led her to believe that he really cared about her. That, even if he hadn't actually said the word, what he felt came close to love, so close that it made no difference. But they had fallen into bed before he had made any sort of declaration—except for that final, darkly triumphant one that had slipped from him when his defences had been down.

What if she had got things terribly wrong?

She had slid carefully from the bed, moving silently so as not to wake Connor, and was pulling on her crumpled clothing, discarded so hastily and with such unthinking carelessness just a few short hours before, when the worst possible scenario finally dawned on her.

'You're not married yet,' Connor had said on the day he had trapped her in the lift with him. 'The wedding isn't until Saturday. That gives me another five days…I reckon that should be more than long enough.'

No!

Jenna clamped a hand over her mouth to catch back the cry of pain that almost escaped her. Had she been the worst sort of a fool imaginable, gullible enough to fall for the cruel scheme of a master manipulator? Was it possible that Connor had meant simply to win her over in order to prove he could?

Was she going to let him take her life in his hands to do what he pleased with it all over again? What evidence did she have that he wasn't just going to while away a few sensual months with her, as he had done five years ago, before the hunger that had gripped him then drove him away to seek newer, more exciting challenges?

Behind her, a clock on the mantelpiece chimed the hour, sending her thoughts into overdrive. She couldn't stay! She had made a promise—a promise that she could never, ever break. What *was* she to do?

A desk in the corner held some of the usual headed notepaper the George provided for its guests. Scribbling frantically, Jenna produced a note in record quick time. If she left it on the coffee table, he was bound to see it. Now she *had* to go!

She was still scrabbling her foot into her second shoe as she fled out into the corridor, heading for the lift.

'Oh, isn't this just the perfect day for a wedding?'

Great-Aunt Millie, resplendent in her wedding finery of bright orange coat and dress, an extravagant cartwheel of silk and tulle crammed on top of her grey curls, was practically dancing with excitement on the pavement outside the church.

'A perfect day for a perfect bride. And you look so beautiful today, my dear.'

'Thank you,' Jenna murmured, smoothing down the white silk skirt of her dress with a hand that was distinctly unsteady, her green eyes anxiously scanning the road beyond the churchyard, looking desperately for the tall, dark, masculine figure she so longed to see.

She knew that the sleek, elegant lines of the dress suited her, flattering her slender height and neat waist, its sweetheart neckline simply hinting at the gentle swell of her breasts. Even the impulsive haircut she had had during the week hadn't ruined things after all. Abandoning the complicated braid, the hairdresser had just caught up her shorter tresses in a loose chignon that looked soft and flattering under the simple head-dress of pink silk rosebuds that matched the posy of the genuine article she clutched in her other, nervously damp hand.

But this morning, as she had dressed in her finery, Jenna had wished herself anywhere but here, doing anything but this. All the while that she had been fielding panic-stricken queries from her mother and sister as to where this was, or what had happened to such and such, her ears had been straining for the sound of a car approaching, the ring of the doorbell.

It hadn't come. And now the hour of the wedding had almost arrived. Nearly everyone was in the church, and

only a few late arrivals, like Great-Aunt Millie, had still to
be shown to their places by the three Kenyon brothers,
resplendent in formal morning dress.

Inside the church the organist was working his way
through the carefully chosen selection of music, waiting for
news of the bride's arrival as the signal to launch into the
traditional fanfare of the 'Wedding March'. And, seated in
the very front pew, his best man at his side, was Graham,
anxiously anticipating the sound of that fanfare that would
announce the end of his bachelor days.

But of Connor there was no sign.

What had happened in that hotel room after she had left?
He must have woken and found her gone. Must have read
the note she'd left.

Jenna bit down hard on her bottom lip, careless of the
way that she was worrying away the soft pink lipstick ap-
plied so carefully only a short time ago. It was either that
or give in to the bitter tears that were swimming in her
eyes, threatening to bring her mascara trickling down her
cheeks.

Had her worst fears been right after all? Had Connor's
only aim been to get her into his bed, and so, he believed,
ruin the prospect of marriage to Graham?

How could she ever get through today if that was true?
How could she endure the ceremony, with its promises of
love and honour, smile at everyone, act as if she hadn't a
care in the world, when all the time her heart was breaking,
shattering into tiny irreparable pieces deep inside her?

'Well, that's everyone seated.' Grant came down the path
towards where she stood at the churchyard gate. 'Time to
go, little sister...'

The rest of his words were drowned by the roar of an
engine, the scream of brakes. Jenna's head swung round,
her heart jumping right up into her throat as she recognised
the car, the dark hair and stunningly attractive face of the
driver.

'Who...?'

Her father had barely time to form the question before
Connor was out of the driving seat, slamming the car door
behind him as he dashed across the road. His eyes were
fixed only on the small group by the churchyard gate, and,
heedless of his own safety, he dodged an oncoming car only
by inches, totally ignoring the blare of its horn as it went
on its way.

'Connor…'

Grant took a step forward, but Connor ignored him.
Vaulting over the wall, he landed just inches away from
Jenna's still form, his blazing blue eyes fixed on her face.

At least he had had a shave, her strained mind noted
with crazy irrelevance. Though not with his usual efficiency. The bright sunlight spotlighted a couple of nicks
where the blood had come to the surface, clear evidence of
the fact that his mind had not been on the job.

His hair, too, had clearly had scant attention, the silky
ebony strands falling in dishevelled disarray so that he
raked them back with a violently impatient hand. He was
wearing one of those impressively tailored dark business
suits that couldn't look anything but elegant if they tried,
but it had obviously been pulled on in frantic haste, as had
the crisp white shirt underneath it. Jenna could see that a
couple of the shirt buttons had been pushed into the wrong
holes, while the jacket hung slightly lop-sided, one shoulder
higher than the other.

The sight of the never less than spruce Connor Harding
in such a state of disarray brought a bittersweet smile to
Jenna's face, one that vanished under the violent onslaught
of his opening attack.

'What the bloody hell sort of game do you think you're
playing?'

'N-no game.'

'Connor…' Grant's voice had a warning note in it.

Connor simply shot him a fiery, scathing glance before
turning his attention back to Jenna. The ferocity of his gaze

stabbed at her, pinning her to the spot as he tugged something from the inside pocket of his jacket.

Behind him, the other Kenyons, mother, father, brother and sister, could only stare in shocked bemusement, completely at a loss as to what was happening.

'Just what is this supposed to mean?'

Shaking open the folded note, which she recognised as the one she had left in his hotel room only that morning, Connor read aloud, his voice shaking with fury.

'''I'm sorry—I really had to go! But I do need to talk to you about the wedding—as soon as possible.'' *Soon!*' he repeated, his tone turning the word into an obscenity. 'How bloody soon, my darling Jenna? Did you plan to talk to me about your wedding after the event? At the reception, perhaps? Or were you thinking of sparing me a couple of minutes while you were on your honeymoon? In between bedding your new husband, or—?'

'It's not like that!' Jenna managed to interject, snatching a moment when he paused for breath.

'Not like that?' Connor echoed with black cynicism. 'Then just what is it like? No.'

A slashing movement of his hand cut her off even before she had begun on a stumbling explanation.

'No, you want to talk, so I'll talk. I'll tell you what I wanted to say to you last night, what I would have said to you this morning if only you'd still been around when I finally woke up. I didn't even stir till midday. And when I did wake, I found *this* ...'

He flung the sheet of paper at her, watching stony-faced as it fell to the ground between them.

'This Dear John letter waiting for me.'

'It's not a Dear John—' Jenna tried again, but he wasn't listening.

His broad chest heaving in a way that had nothing to do with the dramatic rush of his arrival, Connor slowly swung round on his heel, his dark-eyed gaze raking the silent audience of her family. When he came back to face her again he seemed, if not actually calmer, a little more in control. But that control had a fiercely relentless quality that made Jenna shiver in spite of the warmth of the summer afternoon.

'All right,' he said, enunciating the words with a slow precision that was in stark contrast to the wild outpouring of fury that had gone before. 'All right, we'll talk. But I don't think you'll like what I have to say.'

Jenna's father took a hasty step forwards. 'Perhaps this could wait. Or we could leave you...' He let the words drop as Connor shook his head in adamant rejection of them.

'You stay—all of you. I want you to hear this, because I want this damned feud to end here and now—for good.'

Once more he turned his back on their audience, concentrating every bit of his attention on Jenna's pale, strained face. The blue eyes were so deep and dark they were almost black as they held her wide, bewildered emerald ones.

'I have to say this, Jenna, even though it's probably the last thing you want to hear. And I have to say it in front of your family, your parents and your brothers, so that this time there's no possibility of any mistake. I want everyone to know how much I love you.'

Jenna's head went back, a shocked cry catching in her throat. She had to be hearing things. Had Connor said *love*?

'It's more than that—I adore you. You are my life, my heart—my soul! Without you I'm nothing, I'm just existing. My life has no meaning unless you're in it, with me, at my side.'

She should say something, Jenna knew, but no words would form. She could only stare into Connor's impassioned face, struggling to believe that he was actually saying these amazing things.

'And if you feel anything for me, my sweet Jenny Wren, *anything* at all, then you can't go through with this impossible wedding! You can't marry Graham—can't ever be with any other man...'

'Connor...' Jenna managed, hoping to stop him there.

He had said that he loved her, had declared it without fear or hesitation in front of her whole family. What more could she ask?

Her heart was singing, beating a wild, crazy dance under the white bodice of her dress, but she couldn't do anything to express her joy until a couple of basic problems were cleared up.

But Connor was in full flow, determined to say everything that was in his mind, and he would not be stopped.

'You can't do it, Jenny.' His voice had softened now, becoming so gently pleading that it brought swift tears to her eyes. 'It would be so very wrong. Wrong for you to pretend that you can love where you know you can't. Wrong for you to deny your true self, to live your life as a lie—'

'*Connor!*' Jenna broke in more strongly, the sharpness of her tone getting his attention at last. 'This time it's you that's not thinking straight.'

'I'm thinking straighter than at any other time in my life,' Connor declared. 'My mind couldn't be any clearer or more certain. I love you Jenna, and if you're set on marrying Graham—'

'Damn you, Connor!'

This time she actually caught hold of him and gave him an impatient shake, wanting to stamp her feet in frustration.

'Will you *listen* to me? It's not what you think—nothing's as you believe. Use your eyes—please! Look around—look at me!'

Those blue eyes were clouded with confusion, looking bruised and disturbingly vulnerable. He shook his head in bewilderment, sending the soft hair flying over his forehead again.

Swearing fiercely, he raked it back once more, obeying

her instructions and letting his shadowed gaze sweep over her from head to toe, from the delicate head-dress to the dainty satin slippers.

She knew the moment that something registered, because he blinked hard and started the survey again, more slowly this time. At long last she let out the breath she had been holding in and managed a gentle smile.

'Now look over there…'

But this time he was there before her, wheeling round to look more closely at the bridal car parked by the kerb, ribbons fluttering gaily. At the tall figure of Gilbert Kenyon standing beside it, every inch the proud father of the bride in his top hat and tails. And finally, unbelievingly, at the open door of that car.

Inside the Rolls there was a froth of white silk and lace, a bouquet of rich red roses held in delicate feminine hands. A billowing tulle veil held in place by a sparkling tiara partially hid the occupant's face. But even from this distance Connor could recognise the light brown hair and wide blue eyes.

'*Susie!*'

Her sister's name was a choked sound, a cry of shock and disbelief, of a relief so deeply felt that even Jenna's father took pity on him.

'It's my younger daughter I'm giving away today, Connor.'

Jenna too moved forward, and took his hand, unable to leave him in any doubt any longer.

'Connor, it's *Susie's* wedding today, not mine. Sue's the one who's marrying Graham. It was always her, never me.'

Connor's fingers clenched over hers, holding them bruisingly tight. His attention was back on her now, and she could almost hear his mind working, absorbing this new information and processing it.

'Celebrations,' he said slowly. 'You organise parties, birthdays, engagements…that sort of thing.' There was actually a tiny trace of a smile, a lightening of the darkness of his eyes as he quoted her own words back to her. 'And weddings?'

'And weddings,' Jenna admitted, slightly shamefaced. 'This was my special wedding present to Susie. I promised I'd be here for her when she got married. That I would organise her day from start to finish and make it very special for her.'

And one of the things that her sister had wanted was for her one bridesmaid—Jenna—to wear white as well as her. Jenna's dress was a far simpler style, and of course she wore no ornate veil. That and the colour of the roses in her bouquet were what differentiated her from the bride.

'That's why I had to leave you this morning. I'm sorry, Connor.'

But to her surprise Connor was suddenly moving away from her. Striding over the grass verge, he approached the car, crouching down until he was on a level with her sister's wide-eyed gaze.

'Susie, sweetheart, can I beg a very great favour of you? Could I possibly delay your wedding just for five more minutes? I need to borrow your bridesmaid...'

He didn't have to finish. Already Susie was nodding enthusiastically, waving her bouquet in a gesture of dismissal.

'Of course you can, Connor! Take all the time you want. After all, this is supposed to be the happiest day of my life, and I suspect that you could help make it quite perfect.'

Connor blew her a grateful kiss, his face lighting into a vivid smile. Then he sprang to his feet and marched towards where Jenna stood, watching and wondering.

'You and I need a couple of minutes on our own,' he said, snatching up her hand and folding hard fingers around it. 'Come with me.'

She had no choice. Her feet stumbling over the uneven grass, she was pulled along in his wake, around the corner and out of sight behind the church.

'Now...' Connor stopped and swung her round in front

of him, his face set in determined lines. 'I've had my say.
I rather think it's your turn.'

Jenna knew what he wanted, what he needed, and she
had no hesitation in giving it to him.

'Yes, I love you Connor. I always have and I always
will. I may have lost my way a little bit over the past five
years, but deep down I always knew you were the only
man for me.'

She barely had time to get the words out before, with a
groan of pure emotion, he gathered her to him and kissed
her hard.

'You choose your times, you little witch!' he growled
against her mouth. 'Do you know what I would like to do
to you right now?'

Jenna could be in little doubt as to exactly what he
meant. The evidence of his burning physical passion was
crushed, hot and swollen, against the cradle of her hips.

'I think I have a pretty good idea,' she returned pertly,
moving her pelvis against his in a way that brought a moan
of delight from his lips.

'Jenna, behave!' he reproved gently. 'I shall be in enough
trouble with your family as it is for carrying you off like
this. How do you think they'd react if I was to ravish you
here and now, on the grass?'

Teasingly Jenna let her eyes drop to the soft ground that
surrounded them, a wicked gleam lighting in her green
eyes.

'I think Susie might be a little peeved. A bridesmaid with
grass stains all down her dress is definitely not the image
she had planned for her wedding! But I don't think you'd
have to worry about anyone else. If you haven't already
shattered that stupid feud once and for all, I think you'll
find that Grant is now very definitely on your side.'

'Did he ever tell you why he changed his mind?'
Connor's tone had sobered noticeably.

'Yes, he did.' Jenna nodded. 'He said his own experience
of marriage and fatherhood had taught him that love was a

far greater force than hatred any day. He couldn't imagine life without his wife, and because of that he realised what he'd done in trying to keep us apart. Connor...'

But Connor knew what she was trying to say even before she could form the words. He had caught the change in her eyes, the quaver of her voice on the word 'wife', and knew exactly what was going through her mind.

'Let me tell you about my wife, my darling.'

Taking both of her hands in his, he looked deep into her face, his blue eyes wide and clear and open so that she could have no doubts that what he said was the complete truth.

'You were never a substitute for Lucy, Jenny Wren. If anything, poor Lou was a stand-in for you. I couldn't get you out of my mind, and when I met Lucy I thought that perhaps, as you said, I was simply attracted to a type, and any dark-haired, green-eyed beautiful woman would do.'

He shook his dark head in despair at his own foolishness.

'I couldn't have been more wrong. Lucy wasn't anything like you, and she never could have taken your place. The divorce was inevitable; the marriage was doomed from the start. But I felt such a terrible sense of failure, of waste, once the final decree came through. I couldn't shake it off. And I kept coming back to thoughts of you, and that time we spent together. And so I came back...'

'You came back...?'

'Looking for you,' Connor finished for her. 'Why else do you think I was in Greenford? The new store was just a convenient excuse. I'd have come anyway—tried to track you down. And when I saw you that day, at the hotel, I knew that no matter what had happened in the past I still wanted you—more than ever.'

'Because you thought I was going to marry someone else?'

'No.' Once more Connor shook his dark head violently. 'That had nothing to do with it. But I must admit it was something of a shock to the system.'

'I never meant to lie to you...'

'And if I remember rightly, you never actually did,' Connor acknowledged, a glimmer of amused admiration lighting in his eyes. 'After all, I was the one who jumped to the conclusion that when Great-Aunt Millie talked of Saturday's bride she meant you. And, of course, the fact that you were arranging things in your professional capacity made it seem all the more likely that of the two beautiful Kenyon sisters you were the most likely to be the blushing bride. Jenna...?'

'Yes?'

Jenna's heart had started to beat faster than ever. Her eyes were bright with happiness. Connor *loved* her. Connor loved her. It was a glorious refrain inside her head.

Connor loved her, and perhaps now he planned to ask the question that would put the seal on their love, commit them to each other for the rest of their lives.

But instead he pushed back his cuff, consulting the gold watch on his wrist.

'Sweetheart, I would love to stay here alone with you— but I promised Susie only five minutes. We've already overstayed our allotted time, and I would feel terrible if we held up the wedding for any longer, especially as I have one more favour to ask your sister.'

She wouldn't let it bother her, Jenna told herself as, her hand in his, Connor led her back to where everyone else was waiting. She wouldn't let this tiny pinprick spoil her happiness. Hadn't Connor told her that he didn't like to be tied down? And with one ruined marriage already behind him, he would naturally be reluctant to risk such failure ever again.

There had obviously been a hurried family conference while she and Connor were out of sight. Jenna's heart lifted to see the way that, on their return, both her brothers and her father, encouraged by Grant, stepped forward and offered Connor their hands in friendship.

'Welcome to the family.' Gilbert Kenyon's tone was

gruff, but sincere. 'The Kenyon-Harding feud ends right here.'

A few minutes later, all the delays to the wedding were over. After a last tearful kiss for the bride, Penny Kenyon headed for the church on Grant's arm. Connor too, after a whispered conversation with Susie, disappeared inside, and Jenna and her father and sister waited for the music that was their cue to move off down the aisle.

'I'll make sure I throw my bouquet in your direction,' Susie promised, eyes gleaming with excitement, as she took her father's arm.

She didn't believe in such superstitions, Jenna reflected, following them into the church. Catching the bride's bouquet was unlikely to work any special magic. And, if she was honest, did she truly need it? She had Connor's love, his total devotion. What else did anything matter?

But that didn't stop weak tears from pricking at her eyes as she stood behind her sister throughout the ceremony. It didn't stop a pang of longing going through her when Graham placed the ring on Susie's finger and, gently encouraged by the priest, lovingly kissed his new wife.

Connor loves me, she told herself fiercely. To ask for any more would be greedy.

The register had been signed. The wedding was over. It was time for Susie and Graham to leave the church together. So Jenna was stunned and confused when, emerging from the vestry, her sister and brand-new brother-in-law stopped and turned to look at her.

'Jenna...' Susie was urging her forward with a gentle hand on her arm.

'What?' Her bewilderment was total. 'I don't understand...'

'*Look*, silly!' her sister laughed, pointing to the altar where she had taken her vows only a few minutes before.

Jenna looked, blinking in disbelief.

Connor stood at the foot of the altar steps, his face strangely pale and set into taut, uncertain lines. He had managed to sort out the flaws in his appearance during the ceremony. The white shirt was properly buttoned up, the elegant jacket perfectly adjusted. He had even groomed the thick dark hair into sleek smoothness once again.

But that effect was ruined in the moment she turned towards him, as he pushed both hands roughly through the shining strands, ruffling them impossibly. Jenna was stunned to see that his long strong fingers shook perceptibly.

'Go on,' Susie whispered, giving her a none too gentle push forwards.

As Jenna came towards him, on legs that were suddenly drained of all strength, Connor astounded her even more by suddenly going down on one knee on the deep red carpet. Taking her hand very gently in his, he looked up into her mystified face, his eyes the darkest, most intent that she had ever seen them.

'Jenna,' he said, his voice sounding husky and strained, an uncharacteristic hesitancy shading her name. 'Susie and Graham don't mind my usurping their big day for my own ends, and I can think of nowhere better than here, in front of your family and friends, to ask you if you'll help make this glorious day in their lives one of the most wonderful of mine too.'

Jenna found she couldn't breathe, couldn't think. The church she stood in, bright with flowers and candles, the watching congregation filling the pews before her, even her sister and parents at her back, all faded into an incomprehensible blur. Her mind could only focus on Connor's fingers linked with hers, blue eyes locking with green, and his voice saying words she had only ever heard in her dreams before.

'Jenna, darling, please will you make me the happiest man in the world by doing me the honour of becoming my wife?'

Tears of joy sparkled bright as diamonds in Jenna's eyes. Her face was transformed, joy flooding through it as if a powerful, glowing light had just been switched on inside her head.

Dropping her posy unceremoniously onto the floor, she reached out with her free hand to touch his cheek very softly.

'I... I...'

For several dreadful moments she feared that her voice might actually fail her, that she would never be able to get the words out. But then she felt the increased pressure of his hand on hers and swallowed hard to clear the constriction in her throat.

'Oh, Connor, my love, how could I ever say anything but yes?'

Three magnificent millionaires from Down Under—
it's high time they were married!

Meet Tyler, Harry and Val...

The Australian Playboys

in Miranda Lee's racy, sexy new
three-part series.

THE PLAYBOY'S PROPOSITION
#2128
THE PLAYBOY'S VIRGIN
#2134
THE PLAYBOY IN PURSUIT
#2140

*Available in September, October and November in
Harlequin Presents® wherever Harlequin books are sold.*

HARLEQUIN®
Makes any time special ™

Visit us at www.eHarlequin.com

HPTAP

**Don't miss
an exciting opportunity
to save on the purchase of
Harlequin and Silhouette books!**

Buy any two Harlequin or
Silhouette books and save
$10.00 off future Harlequin
and Silhouette purchases

OR

buy any three
Harlequin or Silhouette books
and save **$20.00 off** future
Harlequin and Silhouette purchases.

**Watch for details
coming in October 2000!**

PHQ400

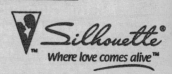